MAGIN

by

Jonathan Day

Dodo Books

CHAPTER 1

Deep in the Hell Well of cosmic implausibilities there was a flurry of movement.

Cloval ignored it. The transmission portal was always throwing up monsters. Even with the obligatory protective field shutting out sights that could turn the mind, the travel technician could tell when they were there, waiting to pounce.

Life was too short to wonder about what was lurking in the depths of the Universe's dungeon. As long as Cloval followed her travel technician's instincts it was unlikely she would encounter one. Doing so would have meant that she had disintegrated and in no state to worry much about it. It's difficult to be devoured by phantoms with your atoms dispersed over light years.

A bio-engineered scout should have been sent through the transmission portal first to check out new destinations. If anything went wrong and the scout was stranded they could easily blend into the target civilisation and avoid any suspicions their sudden appearance might have raised. Tall aliens in gleaming silver protective suits were unlikely to stand a chance.

But this scout was taking too long.

Cloval checked her suit. All trips had to be witnessed by a competent associate. The travel technician, being senior to everyone else and impatient, frequently ignored the procedure. Most people of her age were barred from such risky occupations, and she proved the wisdom of this rule with her unbounded unpredictability.

Cloval always started with the intention of behaving herself and checked over the recall unit that had to go through the transmission portal with the scout. Without it, return from the Hell Well would have been impossible.

The longer Cloval waited, the greater the temptation became. She had broken safety protocols before and survived and this new, alien wonderland was just one step into infinity away. Her colleagues were aware of their superior's reputation and that she should never have been left alone in the transmission control, but they were all too busy somewhere else.

Cloval's impatience went into overdrive and resentment kicked in. Why should only scouts have first sight of the worlds her team had worked so hard to establish a link with? They were genetically manipulated non-entities without a point of view. How could they appreciate momentous occasions like this?

The bolts securing her commonsense thrown back, Cloval programmed the co-ordinates to that tempting, small blue planet, and opened the shutter to the Hell Well. After another brief check of her suit, she braced herself to encounter the forces that would dismantle her atom by atom and drop her into that chasm of alternative dimensions filled with monsters from the Universe's subconscious.

But it was one drop into an alternative reality too many.

There was another reason old age was regarded as a liability - Cloval had forgotten to take the recall unit with her.

CHAPTER 2

The sunlight danced in the crystal facets of the overhead glass like a swarm of demented fireflies. The tall, lean man gazing up at his triple glazed ceiling sometimes felt as though he was living at the bottom of a transparent sea encrusted with ice. He always felt cold; frosty fingers clutched his heart, even when the sun was at its zenith.

Magin stretched indolently and reached for the button to read his mail. His life was lived in such secrecy he seldom had much. As usual, there was a message from his surgeon reminding him to look after this implant or another; an admonishment that would no doubt carry on throughout his lifetime. There was also a message from the surgeon's son scolding him for not attending some important function. Oh, the innocence of the young. Whenever the agent arrived at any function, heads turned as if the devil had walked in and immediately undermined his undercover status.

But the last message meant an end to the preposterous games he was obliged to play in high society's gatherings, being introduced as the person trained to encounter aliens. His expertise was at last being called upon. There was no one else to do it and his superiors were panicking.

On a planet with air so cold, birds had not evolved, someone who should have known better had opened the corridor into space-time - and forgotten to take the key. Magin was the only one who could track them down before other agencies managed to.

CHAPTER 3

Thumper sliced a piece from the firm grey clay. She threw it with more vigour than was necessary onto the revolving wheel and reduced it to a glutinous slurry with handfuls of water and post examination relief. She no longer needed to turn complicated teapots or press white clay into wafer thin porcelain bowls. Now was the time to paint abstract patterns onto coarse pots and coil chunky vases.

Veronica had always grudgingly accepted that her fellow student was the most talented of her class, the only one able to sell enough work to pay for her keep. Thumper's was so good, her Aunt Daffy was going to allow her to use the garden shed for a second-hand potter's wheel and the electric kiln the bank was granting her a loan for.

Veronica sighed enviously. Aunt Daffy was as eccentric as her niece and always let her have her own way. Thumper's academic mother had decided that her scruffy daughter would be better off living with her sister-in-law

3

after her younger offspring announced on her tenth birthday the intention of sailing to Japan to study pots. Aunt and niece were like minds. Daffy could have either talked her out of it or built a raft and gone with her. It wouldn't have been so bad if Thumper had chosen her mother's continent, Africa. Women there knew more about making pots than some Japanese mystic with a feeling for clay.

Uhura Dillinger had never understood her daughter. Thumper was the child Daffy should have had. Uhura understood her husband even less, and left him to teach computer studies in her home town. Thumper received the occasional photograph of a zebra, pot or star pupil: more than she got from her remarried father and older brother.

Thumper's clay slowly spun to a halt and she began to pinch ornate ribs into its sides. She completed the monstrosity by dribbling a tracery of slip into its bowl.

Veronica gazed at the creation in disbelief, wondering why such a consummate craftswoman would want to make such a ghastly object. 'What on earth is it?'

'A dog dish.'

'Another one?'

'The decent ones get broken. Rascal flings them across the kitchen. It's her way of complementing the chef.'

'Why not get her a tin one?'

Thumper sneered. 'Tin? How can you expect any living creature to eat out of tin?'

'Tupperware then?'

'What's that?'

Veronica didn't answer. It was unlikely Thumper and her aunt frequented the retro junk shops her mother was addicted to.

'How many dogs has your aunt got now?'

'Oh - fifteen or seventeen - or so.'

'They must cost a fortune?'

'They do. She gets a small grant from a charity to supplement her works pension.'

Veronica gingerly set her fragile model of a pixie's house on a stand to dry. 'Seen Eccles lately?'

'Couple of weeks ago. She's working on a relief and I helped her unload some stone from the quarry.'

'Beats me how she manages to wield a chisel with her rheumatism.'

'Doesn't bother her that much now. Most of the modelling she does is for casting anyway.'

'Did she ever get around to trying lost wax?'

'Yes. Her foundry buggered it up. The mould wasn't strong enough.'

'Must be wonderful for filigree work.' Veronica sat back, admired her model, and dreamt of the angel hair and fairy wings which could be fired - or shattered - in the new kiln.

Thumper knew what her friend was thinking. 'Every other thing you put into the kiln falls apart.'

'Well, they always fire things at the wrong temperature at the college.'

Thumper knew what she was driving at. 'Oh, all right. You find out what the right temperature is, and I'll let you have the odd firing in my kiln when it's installed.'

'Really?' Veronica bounced up so enthusiastically her plaits lashed through the air and nearly knocked the roof off her creation. 'I know you don't really think much of my little ornaments.'

This took Thumper aback. 'I've never said that.' Perhaps she paid so little attention to the other students' work that they all had that impression. When she wasn't so self-absorbed, the range of glazes, textures, and even fairy filigree her fellow students created often impressed her. Their work would never sell, apart from Veronica's. Her work was twee enough to be popular. All she needed was a firm, guiding hand.

'There's quite a market for fairy falderals. Your main problem is getting it out of the kiln intact enough to sell.'

'You can really be thoughtful sometimes, Thumper.'

'How d'you mean?' Thumper thought she had sounded

too condescending to merit thanks.

'Well, you're not as hard as you sometimes make out.' Veronica scrubbed her hands in the sink and rubbed in enough hand cream for a body massage. 'Be in tomorrow?'

'Don't know. Old Walcott said it doesn't matter and he's only having the kiln on once a week now. I'm up to my limit as it is. I'm getting a lot of stuff fired over at The Pottery. They bought another batch of our mugs last week.'

'Great.'

'And the Hollybush will let us have a cheque at the end of the month.' Thumper was thoughtful for a moment. 'Veronica ..?'

Veronica was already listening intently and desperately trying not to show it.

'Ever thought about us going into business together? I mean - properly?'

'Why not? We can sell all the mugs we make.' Veronica tried to sound a little diffident, but enthusiasm leeched out of every syllable.

'It'll be easier when I get the kiln of course.'

'I'd put the money I make into the business until we're in profit.'

'So will I.' Thumper was surprised at how painless it was to set up a serious partnership. 'That's okay then?'

'Sure.'

'Great.' Thumper suddenly found that she was unable to close the conversation.

Brimming with excitement, Veronica took the initiative. 'I'll make sure Mr Walcott fires all your stuff if you aren't in tomorrow.'

'Thanks.'

Having to find someone to tell before she exploded, Veronica pulled on her jacket and darted out to the college canteen.

Thumper was plunged into thought about the persona she apparently intimidated the rest of the class with. "Hard"? Never. Perhaps a little outspoken by their insipid standards. The cutting edge of her tongue could be a little too accurate at times - but hard?

She sliced the dog bowl from the wheel, put it on a rack to dry, and then dutifully mopped up the worst of the slip so the room was reasonably tidy for Mr Michael's evening class. The white fingerprints on the cupboard doors and occasional bullet of clay adhering to the windows had raised comments from some of his pupils more used to semi-detached domestication. Thumper hated their middle class normality. Its hypocrisy had ruined her parent's marriage. She was convinced that the influential hitched a comfortable ride through life at the expense of those who felt obliged to abide by their oppressive conventions. That's why she was living with Aunt Daffy in her acre of orchards and vegetable plots, rescuing unwanted dogs and writing letters of complaint to supermarkets, institutions and utility companies who could only be dealt with over the Internet. Her aunt found gratification in technophobia, making offices that depended so much on e-mail to write letters and pay for a stamp. Thumper was lucky; her trade didn't depend on having a website, and a decent kiln was more important than a computer. Her brother was the one who always had a mobile phone to his ear, which probably accounted for his weak intellect.

Scooping up the unused clay, Thumper hurled a clod of it with uncharacteristic malice into the reclaim bin at the thought of her brother, another for her mother, and the largest for her father. She slammed the lid and sealed it.

After washing the clay from her hands and arms, she gathered up her ancient duffle bag and wandered along to the college canteen to collect a chocolate bar and cup of tea. Veronica and a cluster of friends had already left to celebrate her new business venture with decent cappuccinos at her mother's favourite restaurant. To Thumper, one drink out of an oblong, aluminium dispenser tasted very much like another, and she was happy to refresh herself with the powdered concoction dribbled from the canteen coffee machine. Then she persuaded one of the junior students to help her load the pottery she had amassed in her locker over the past term into the boot of her Mini.

On the way home, Thumper stopped on Shoreham Ridge to watch the descending summer sun pattern the fields below with lengthening shadows. She wondered why she couldn't revel in the beauty of the scene. Veronica would have pulled out a pencil and pad from her neat little knapsack to dash off lines of poetry. Perhaps Thumper's genius for handling material that came out of the ground barred her from appreciating the vistas above it. Did that make her hard, though? This was something she would have to sort out before she became an adult and too self-important to bother.

Thumper sighed. How she wished she could meet someone, apart from Aunt Daffy, who understood her. It could have scales and tentacles for all she cared, because it was unlikely to be the world's most glamorous man.

Pulling the last sandwich from her duffle bag, she sat on the brow of the hill and wondered what it would be like to live on another planet with exotic minerals just waiting to be mined, sculpted and turned. Perhaps there would be quartz the texture of biscuit, glittering like trays of diamonds, obsidian which could be sliced to reveal veins of rare metals, or granite shot through with glasses smelted in the fires of an alien furnace or sandwiched by the volcanic forces of Io. No, that moon was mainly sulphur. Venus perhaps. Just the right gravity for making rock sandwiches and an atmosphere which could melt concrete.

Oh, the wonders in the Cosmos she would never know. Thumper would have to be content with the interminable seasons that cloaked the countryside in predictable pastel colours year after year. Even sulphur had a better idea of what yellow should be than a buttercup.

Thumper wondered what it would be like to live in the land of her mother's African ancestors, not the mild, misty rural world of her father. The potter had an amazing rapport with dogs, so it was unlikely a few lions would bother her. She wanted village women to teach her how to make huge, thin-shelled storage jars with strips of clay and how to fire them on an open hearth. Perhaps she should join her mother? But she lived in a town that spoke Yoruba. And all those jabs she would need - malaria, elephantiasis, beriberi, rabies... What Thumper wanted was... she didn't really know. She would soon leave college with the best qualifications, her own business, and a second hand car. That should have been enough.

Thumper swallowed the rest of the pickle sandwich and sat with her chin on her knees until the sinking sun cast its rosy hue. Satisfied that it looked sufficiently mineral and all was well with the world after all, she got back into her Mini and drove home.

CHAPTER 4

Magin again glanced at his instructions. He hadn't expected them to be contained in an encrypted file even he had difficulty decoding. At least it offered a welcome relief from his confined life.

So, what clothes would be suitable for this bizarre mission? Should he be immaculate, the severe front of authority, or more casual to reassure the obdurate locals he was bound to encounter? Perhaps he should opt for the intimidating, just to be on the safe side. He did that very well without even trying, which was odd. He had never considered his unusual appearance or mellow tones to be unfriendly. Perhaps it was just a bonus that he shouldn't question in his line of work.

Now, what sort of intimidation to opt for? Clean cut correctness? No, perhaps Magin should just be himself - as far as his carefully manufactured identity would allow anyway. Given what he was being told to do, appearance hardly mattered.

Magin picked up the instructions and took them to another room where he didn't feel as though the Universe was spying on him through his triple glazed ceiling.

This was a mission he may not return from. It was not something he had ever taken into account before. He was surprised to discover that it didn't really bother him.

He wondered why.

CHAPTER 5

Hollybush Ceramics and Handicraft Shop was so old it had centuries of grime ingrained in beams low enough to decapitate the average 20th century male. The heads of its owner and Thumper were well below that risk.

Thumper gasped. 'How many mugs?' Her hand hovered over the order book as she calculated the amount of work involved. Throwing the mugs was no problem; it was painting the decorative falderals. Thank God for Veronica.

Mrs Knight smiled. 'You can manage two hundred, can't you? I won't need them until Christmas. That gives you over five months.'

'So when do you want the plant holders?'

'As soon as possible. Special order.' Mrs Knight rummaged in a drawer and pulled out a letter. 'I'll give you the logo. Very fussy. Must be exact.'

Thumper looked at the meticulous letter heading. 'Can't guarantee the plants he puts in them will all trail to the same length.'

'Well, you know what those upmarket hotels are like. Can you match this glaze?' She handed Thumper a photo.

'Have to experiment.' Thumper rubbed the square of sienna fabric pinned to it. 'Nice velvet.'

'Costs a week's wages to stay one night there. I couldn't find anyone local to do the macramé pot hangers. Had to send the order to London.'

'Aunt Daffy can crochet.'

'You couldn't get that amount of silk locally.'

Thumper whistled.

'And would a vegetarian agree to working in it?'

'Given the amount of meat she prepares for the dogs, I couldn't see that bothering her.' Thumper flipped back through her order book. 'How did the other mugs go?'

'Three of the decorated ones left. I've still got a dozen of the plain.'

'Philistines.'

'People like Veronica's busy little decorations. They buy them for presents. Has she agreed to go into business with you?'

'As soon as I get the kiln. Her stuff needs to be fired carefully. The old furnace at the college shatters all her angel hair and pretty flowers. At the moment we spend most of the profit on firings at The Pottery, and Aunt Daffy won't let me make my own kiln.'

Thumper kept telling her aunt that the shed was too damp to burn, but she had this thing about running anything on a high voltage and Veronica's ornaments wouldn't have survived the bonfire she wanted to experiment with - not that aunt Daffy would have let her light that either. Though she could only get a loan for a small kiln that used power economically, it would mean firing every night and her paying the electric. But they could get enough advance orders to make it worth while, and The Pottery promising to take anything at cost if they couldn't get rid of it. Veronica also wanted to stop on at college for another year to do accounting, and Thumper toyed with the idea of trying her hand at wood turning and carpentry. It would work fine unless Veronica decided to follow the family tradition and raise a typical middle class, dysfunctional family. Though after the divorce, she would probably come back. The only family Thumper ever wanted was Aunt Daffy and the dogs.

The potter took a small carving of an angel down from a cluttered shelf. 'Unusual wood?'

'Padauk. It's bright orange when it's first cut, then darkens. Difficult to carve, but old Alice has a way with a chisel which dumfounds me.'

'Pity she never does anything larger.'

'Has trouble getting the exotic woods and her husband
don't like the vice clamped to the kitchen table. I've sold
everything she's brought in so far. Offered to let her use
the back room, but she doesn't like being away from the
chickens with that fox on the prowl.'

Thumper replaced the angel and browsed along the
shelves crammed with craftwork from local people and
irresistible trinkets from India and China.

Her gaze settled on a shell necklace. 'I've never seen
cowries that colour before?'

'They come from the Philippines.' Mrs Knight took it
down and put it round Thumper's neck. 'Suits you.'

'How much?'

'Nothing. It's been hanging there for long enough. I
thought about making a shell box with it, but it seemed a
shame to break it up.'

'You sure?'

'Try firing some porcelain brooches for me. I'll take one
of them in exchange.'

'OK.'

'Not sunflowers or Venus fly traps though. Primroses or
violets.'

'I'll consult Veronica.'

After choosing a small pillbox for her ex tutor, Eccles,
Thumper left to meet her for coffee, and ruminate over
the new order in her pad. She would need more plaster
and glaze, and to install her second-hand wheel within
the next two weeks.

Thumper was on her second cup by the time Eccles
arrived. The sculptor was a large-framed, rugged woman
and showed few signs of the encroaching rheumatism that
was trying to ravage her joints. After tutoring during
Thumper's first year at college she had settled on the
coast and only came inland for the odd visit to a
physiotherapist. Her teaching was now limited to evening
classes.

'How's things?' Eccles croaked. She dropped her knapsack onto the chair next to Thumper and lit a cigarette.

'Not bad.' Thumper pointed diplomatically to the cafe's "No Smoking" sign.

Eccles threw a window open and held her cigarette over the pavement outside.

The waitress took the eccentric's occasional visits in her stride. 'Usual?'

'Yes. In a mug. Without milk. Thanks.'

'How did the casting for that Newmarket stable go?' asked Thumper.

'Fine, fine. Installed it a week ago. Makes the horses shy, but the owner likes it.'

'How was the physio?'

'Same as before. Keeps nagging me to stay out of the damp.'

'Why don't you move inland?'

'I'd never find light like that anywhere else.'

Thumper pulled the pillbox from her duffle bag. 'Something to keep your tablets in.'

Eccles took it with a smile that should have been carved on a totem pole. 'Just the job. Keep losing bottles. Thanks. How's your Aunt Daffy?'

'Same. Still as batty as ever.'

'Dogs?'

'Two more. A Jack Russell and ginger bottle brush.'

The waitress came over with a mug and plate of biscuits. 'One lapsang and ginger nuts. Anything else?'

'No thanks.' Eccles tossed her cigarette out of the window. It bounced off a pigeon pecking its way through a squashed tomato sandwich donated by an earlier customer. 'Seen any gorillas lately?'

'Only fur fabric ones.'

'Got a beauty to cast next month. Pity he only wants a bust. His arms reach his knees.' The sculptor pulled a sketchpad from her knapsack.

Thumper wondered if she would ever get paid if her

clients found out what she said about them.

Eccles scribbled away in the pad for a few moments. 'When are you coming out to see me then?'

'It's half a day's drive. Not sure the Mini's up to it.'

'Bosh. If it can't make the round trip, I can always hitch it to the back of the station wagon and tow you back.'

'Don't the police ever stop that thing?'

'Only to marvel. Mostly leaves them standing.'

'Don't suppose they often hear the engine of a centurion tank under the bonnet of a car.'

'Don't exaggerate. The original engine and axle would never have been able to take the weight of the stone.'

'Why didn't you buy a truck instead?'

'Old ladies driving trucks do get stopped by the police.'

Thumper laughed. 'Well, I suppose we're all aliens to someone.'

'Nonconformists always are.'

Thumper looked at Eccles' sketch of layered red streaks. 'What's that?'

'Best sunrise I ever saw. Two morning ago.'

'Bet you can't sculpt it.'

'You can be an adolescent prat at times. How old are you?'

'Twenty at Christmas and should be earning a living.'

'Well when you're qualified, don't you dare become a teacher. It'd be taken bread out of the mouths of those poor souls not fit for anything else.'

'I'll wait till I'm your age and let someone invite me.'

Eccles swallowed her tea, put some change on the table and rose. 'Have to go now. Got to get to the foundry before the treatment wears off. Don't forget to come out some time. Gets boring talking to herring gulls.' Hurling her knapsack over her shoulder, the sculptor strode off as though she had never had a muscle twinge in her life.

CHAPTER 6

The travel technicians in Cloval's team should have been awed at the enormity of manipulating the very fabric of the Universe. Tampering with quantum anomalies required a detached state of mind, so detached, they could to look into the jaws of Hell and not turn to stone. So when Cloval disappeared through yet another portal into an unknown corner of the Cosmos, no one was unduly worried at first. The absence of her intimidating, impatient presence was to be savoured for as long as possible. She had lived long enough to give every one of them reason for grief, so her immediate rescue was not uppermost in their minds and they had been reluctant to risk a valuable scout. They were not easily replaced if anything happened to them. Fortunately, the one designated for this planet wasn't yet a star in the auditoriums where the Sovariagn population swarmed to learn how other species went about their strange, alien lives. Its mission would remain secret and out of the embarrassing scrutiny of the movement canvassing to put an end to their expensive enterprise. It was also certain that none of Cloval's travel technicians were going to volunteer to jump into a wildly fluctuating portal to rescue their bad-tempered associate.

Even on Sovariagn, that would have been an altruism too far.

So, reluctantly, they had contacted Monitor Forram requesting the relevant scout, an untested unit none of them had set eyes on it before. Usually, the technicians had time to assess its appearance, limitations, and have a secret sneer at its alien characteristics. There was no opportunity this time. Monitor Forram's star pupil only had a short briefing before being suspended over that well looking straight down into the basement of a churning cosmic hell.

This was not a region of matter, compressed or otherwise, but tangle of cosmic possibilities. Teasing out the exact possibility and making it tangible was an art the Sovariagn jealously kept from their neighbours. This technology was created for their planet-bound species. Those who could travel space had no need to look into the maws of a portal where so many possibilities, fluid and half-formed, could turn the sanest of minds. Though they may have been a little unhinged, even the travel technicians avoided looking into it, apart from Cloval who they suspected was already mad before she joined the unit. They preferred to monitor its activity through a surveillance system that shielded them from the distortion. Their most important function was to relay enough information from target planets to the experts encoding the languages and, more importantly, creating credible creatures to resemble and sound like their inhabitants. Theirs was a secretive department and few questioned how they went about their vital work of bioengineering the scouts destined to travel through the Hell Well, and hopefully return to relate their experiences. They were trained to step into the transmission chamber without wearing the highly reflective suits that created a force field to prevent exposure to the dungeon dimensions of the universe. Cloval, the only technician prepared to jump into the transmission stream and donate her atoms to dangerous, unknowable implausibilities, had always come back in one piece. A little madder perhaps, but that came of having the atoms of her brain converted into tachyon waves once too often.

When the scout arrived, it was quite calm about the prospect of being transmitted through the Hell Well to an alien world to retrieve Cloval. It didn't utter a sound as a Monitor Forram fastened a narrow transmission collar round its neck. There was still a chance that Cloval hadn't already been seen and picked up. If the highly trained Sovariagn technicians found this scout unnervingly strange, they didn't like to think what the planet would make of Cloval.

CHAPTER 7

Thumper would have stayed in bed until eight o'clock if
Aunt Daffy's dogs hadn't started to bark loud enough to
wake the neighbourhood. There were a couple of locals
who would appreciate any excuse to have her kennels
closed down, so Thumper pulled on some jeans and a T-
shirt to find out what had set the dogs off. There were one
or two hardened howlers refusing to quieten down;
fortunately many of the others were now cringing in the
shed and under the stairs like menaced rabbits. Each dog
had its own idiosyncrasy, so it wasn't often they all
decided to bark at the same time.

Only Porky and Pine, the porcupines, on their worst
behaviour could drive the dogs that crazy and both of
them had been sleeping in Thumper's bedroom. They
joined her as she climbed through the fence into the
grounds of the neighbouring, large estate.

The only suspicious thing she found was some odd
fungi which turned out to be a couple of golf balls that
looked as though they had been chewed up by the Hound
of the Baskervilles. Like most people searching for
something, it didn't occur to her to look up. There was the
sound of dogs and police cars coming from a distant lane.
More than one policeman in the area was something of a
novelty, more than one car full - and dogs - must have
meant that whatever was prowling the district had form.

Cloval peered down at the strange creature through the
branches of her tree. It was difficult to sum up what was
normal for a human with her Sovariagn perceptions. The
creature's appearance seemed scruffy, but it was well
thought out, like a weed with a sense of style. Her species
prided itself on being immaculate so Thumper was
difficult to place on the ladder of otherworldliness.

Without makeup or easily defined waistline, she would
have been amazed and gratified to know an alien found
her such an enigma. Thumper resembled her Aunt Daffy.
They had both achieved the impossible for most people by

being satisfied with themselves the way they were. Thumper often used to wear her brother's old football socks whenever he switched allegiance, and keep her long, frizzy hair out of her eyes with strands of melon seeds and bugle beads. The resulting tangles eventually cured her of the habit.

Conformity to Thumper was jeans, T-shirts or flounced cheesecloth blouses, backless Dutch clogs and a tartan poncho found in a charity shop. Like the true eccentric, Thumper was totally unaware she was one.

As she passed out of Cloval's view, the alien would have been alarmed to know that the human was heading towards the small pavilion where the Sovariagn transmission portal was located.

At last the distant howling of the dogs died away, so whatever was a bothering them must have gone. It was probably only a fox. There had been the odd sighting of a big cat over the years, but no one had ever found its spoor or paw prints. Thumper had always assumed it to be someone's overfed moggie.

It was too late to go back to bed, so she went up the crumbling steps into the folly that had been built by the first owners of the country estate and fought back the temptation to heave away the lid reclining solidly on a granite bowl too massive to be of any use. For over a century the Victorian monstrosity had sat on the flagstones of the pavilion's floor, defying its Georgian elegance and waiting for some superhuman youth to come along and vandalise it.

Thumper failed to see what purpose it could have served. It was too monstrous, even for the Victorians, to inter anyone's ashes. Not unless it had been intended for their bones after a respectable time in the charnel house, which would explain the weight of the lid; or there might have been the booty of a villain who hid his treasure inside it before ending up on the gallows. Or perhaps there were steps down to a subterranean tunnel leading to the huge scullery of the empty manor house.

Thumper often found the Victorian sense of art difficult to distinguish from the Victorian sense of humour. Planting such an uncompromising lump of granite in the middle of an elegant Georgian folly had to be irony. The only other explanation was that it had been installed by the patriarchal head of a large female brood in the hope that some unsuspecting Pandora would come along and break her varnished fingernails in an effort to prize it open. Thumper's well-chewed nails hardly qualified. It was virtually impossible to throw pots with spikes at the end of each finger. Yet again, it might have been put there to obstruct the consummation of any illicit nocturnal assignation.

Thumper told herself to stop fantasising. There was only one way to solve the riddle that had baffled her from infancy. If she could just nudge that lid aside a fraction to take a quick glimpse inside...

No one was watching. Even Porky and Pine were more interested in rummaging through the weeds overgrowing the pavilion steps.

Thumper ran her fingers around the rim of the lid to find a handhold. Without industrial pollution, the granite had remained as smooth as when the mason had first polished it.

She slapped the dressed grey stone in frustration. It was only a light smack - a broken wrist was no use to a potter - but she felt the lid move. To her amazement it was floating a millimetre above the vase's rim, buoyed up by some mysterious force like a linear train. This wasn't granite; the carved aggregate was behaving like polystyrene.

Thumper's senses had to be deceiving her so she pushed the lid just enough to peer into the bowl.

As her nose drew level with the rim, the lid suddenly hurtled into the air.

She ran for her life down the steps as it crashed into the weeds the porcupines had been rummaging through only seconds before.

By the time Thumper had plucked up enough courage to go back and investigate Porky and Pine were halfway home.

The potter peered apprehensively into the huge granite bowl, fully expecting some fire breathing dragon to be nesting inside it. There was nothing. The rough interior suggested that the granite container had never been intended to open in the first place.

The grounds of the estate had become so run down by the agents of the owners they would probably not notice the dislodged lid. They were more concerned about the valuable antiques in the manor house.

Thumper glanced about uneasily.

She would have followed Porky and Pine if she hadn't noticed someone watching her.

A tall, slender man was standing on the wide sweep of stone steps leading down to the estate's grand avenue.

One of the man's hands rested on the ornamental balustrade and the other was held rigidly behind his back. Too disconcertingly distinguished to be young, he had the straight-limbed poise of a guardsman. Silhouetted against the distant manor house, he could have been its aristocratic owner, a wicked squire who terrorised the neighbourhood until dragged down to Hell by the Devil. Thumper didn't usually conjure up such images from Hammer Horror films or Mozart operas, but there was something sinister about this stranger.

Against her better judgement, Thumper approached him.

The man's dark, amber eyes had a satanic gleam like a guttering candle's flame, and there was a brittle remoteness about him, like a piece of delicate porcelain or spiny scorpion fish, only to be viewed and certainly not touched. His ivory toned skin was clean-shaven and would have blended into the turtle neck of his light-coloured shirt had his jaw line not been so firm. A collarless black frock coat, two glinting gem fastenings pinning it to his elegant figure, complemented the dense colour and cut of his hair. He was clean cut, polished intimidation itself.

Thumper cast him a quick smile. 'Afternoon.' Having scrutinised him so thoroughly she had to say something and would have strode steadily away, not expecting, or wanting, a reply.

Escape wasn't that easy, though.

'Good afternoon.' The stranger had a rich, measured tone that made her hesitate from taking another step. 'May I ask if you live locally?'

'Yeah.' Thumper sensed she would rue the moment hadn't kept walking.

He wasn't discouraged by her calculated lack of response. 'Perhaps you could help me? I am investigating the sighting of something strange.'

Thumper may have only recently been a teenager, but she could place people's occupations as well as identifying stone by its weight and texture. 'You're not a copper.' Then it clicked. That was why the police dogs were out there. They were probably after the same thing. In their locality, more than one manhunt would have been a coincidence too far.

'Is it that obvious?'

'I'm a good guesser.'

Behind his raised eyebrow he might have been agreeing with the scruffy young woman. 'Are you local?'

Thumper wanted to get away from the interloper. 'What do you need to know for? You recruiting for some weird Jesus cult?'

'I'm sure someone with your strength of character has no reason to fear being taken in by them.'

Thumper's hackles rose. It was a reasonable observation, but the man's cool, self-assurance made it sound like an insult.

'Who are you?' she demanded.

He lifted a monogrammed handkerchief to his upper lip with unconvincing affectation. 'Any alien creature accidentally stranded here could well find this heat uncomfortable, don't you think?'

'Uncomfortable?' Thumper was half African. It was just a balmy, warm day. Then she realised what he had said. 'Alien?'

It occurred to her that he was enjoying the encounter too much. 'Get a life.'

'You haven't noticed any aliens then?'

'For pity's sake...' Hardly were the words out of her mouth when she realised that he must have seen her and the granite lid doing their novelty turn.

In a second of weakness, she glanced back at the pavilion, but it was too early in the morning to deal with something this weird. Her interest in the occult, conspiracies, and unexplained didn't usually warm up until much later. In a few hours time, she could handle smoothness incarnate, but she needed breakfast first.

Strengthening her resolve, she walked away. 'I'm not hanging about unless you've got some ID on you.'

'Perhaps we'll meet again.' He gave a smile so charismatic it must have been rehearsed.

Without another word, Thumper dashed off before curiosity compelled her to glance back.

The man remained standing to attention, watching her with cool bemusement.

'Tell your aunt that her dogs should not be disturbed much longer,' he called after her.

Thumper mouthed an obscenity at him. She should have been too far away for him to make out what it was.

The raised eyebrow announced otherwise.

After she had gone he remained as motionless as the redundant telegraph poles that straddled the domed horizon of meadowland. The previous owner of the estate had lost her battle to stop them being erected. Her nephew got his own back by refusing to let anyone take them down. So there they stood, slowly rotting; pronged perches for flocks of roosting starlings. The urgent messages that had once been transmitted along their lines were probably as complex and varied as the thoughts going on behind the stranger's impassive features.

Thumper now well out of sight, Magin gazed at the
swifts scything through the clear sky as though silently
counting the greenfly being gathered in their gaping
beaks.

He slipped off his long frock coat to luxuriate in the
warm breeze. The popular perception of a secret agent
might have had him stalking some network of
fluorescently lit corridors, driving fast cars or tailing other
agents through blankets of night time drizzle. Magin was
too complex to fit such a stereotype.

Then he turned his attention to the lid of the granite
vase.

Thumper wasn't easily alarmed. She was usually the
one to unsettle other people. This time she had met her
match.

Barking announced her arrival well before she reached
the house, and as soon as she entered the front door she
was greeted by dogs of various shapes and sizes.

'Aunt Daffy!' she called from under the hairy reception
committee.

Her aunt came from the kitchen clutching a tin opener
in one hand and lemon in the other. 'Where have you
been?'

'I need a drink.' Thumper was thrown from what she
was about to blurt out when she noticed that Aunt Daffy
had somehow managed to peel half the lemon with the tin
opener. 'What are you doing?'

'I need a decent blade. Not as badly as you need a drink
by the sound of it though.'

Thumper automatically reached down to her belt and
unclipped her penknife. 'What happened to the vegetable
knife?'

'Down the back of the sink unit with the other four and
none of the cutlery's sharp enough. There isn't a blade left
capable of cutting butter. You'll have to get inside the
shed and find what I did with the whetstone. There's a
stout in the kitchen.'

The momentum to spill out her story now totally lost,

Thumper followed her.

Daffy's house was large. It needed to be to accommodate umpteen dogs and two orphaned porcupines. There was still the faint smell of wood treated for dry rot. This competed with the distinctive aroma of damp dog in the hall where the more boisterous ones were confined until dry enough to be allowed into the other rooms. It meant that the rest of the house by comparison smelt sweet.

There was a high gate only a desperate Great Dane could have jumped, barring canine entry to the stairs. As well as the upper floors, the dogs were not allowed near the cold storage unit in the kitchen. That contained six months of dog rations and the store of last autumn's fruit and veg of neighbours without a deep-freeze. The vet had commented that it was the largest domestic freezer he had ever strolled into, not able to make her admit that it had originally been purloined by a team of poachers from a bacon factory that had gone into sudden liquidation. She had to have it, though, and storing the neighbours' produce helped subsidise its running cost. Daffy didn't like handling meat, but until she could persuade the dogs to become vegetarians, there was little she could do about it.

'Blew into the air? A lump of granite?' Daffy exclaimed through a moustache of stout foam. 'What did it do that for?'

Thumper sighed. 'Beats me.'

'It was probably the wind, dear.' Daffy swallowed the rest of her stout, and then started to slice carrots.

'Like the way it's been upsetting the dogs?'

'The wind can play funny tricks. It lifted the thatch from one of the old cottages before they were pan tiled.'

'That's because it hadn't been tied down well enough. I don't think that character in the frock coat and demonic haze believes he's only looking for a freak effect of the wind. Dead sinister he is.'

'Might be the new vicar of St Anne's. They say he's

quite trendy.'

'I didn't notice which way up he was wearing his crucifix.'

Daffy was more interested in chopping carrots than the new vicar. She was the last person a clergyman would visit.

Thumper rambled on, 'Though, come to think of it, he was wearing a gold pendant, and I'm pretty sure he wasn't looking for lost sheep... extraterrestrial ones perhaps... What are you making?'

'Carrot pie.'

By the size of the dish, Thumper knew she was going to get to know it very well over the next few days.

CHAPTER 8

As dusk fell Cloval came down from her tree now the air was much cooler. She had lost the feeling in most of her extremities by crouching so long, out of sight, in its cleft branches. Her silver suit still glinted annoyingly, so Cloval made for the cover of some bushes. Small animals scurried away and a bolder fox watched the alien from a safe distance. The technician had never encountered a moth before, now swarms of them mistook her for a lamp.

Brushing the annoying insects away and hoping that their emanations weren't toxic, Cloval began to make calculations on her monitor. Without the benefit of an icy breeze and having to keep an eye on the eyes glowing in the shadows, she found it annoyingly laborious and had to repeat them several times.

Her conclusions weren't encouraging: all any search party would find of her if she was stuck in this place for long enough, was a silver suit filled with interesting biological goo. She toppled back with heat exhaustion and landed in some brambles. It was like being mauled by a many-tentacled predator. Cloval was more than a match for anything with teeth and flew into a rage. The thorns took fright and immediately released her.

The technician would have to find shelter safer than a tree, which she was bound to fall out when she collapsed of heatstroke. It would have to be before the light was totally gone: on her planet night never fell.

There was nothing for it but to take a risk.

Cloval broke cover and darted towards the portal in the pavilion, her explosion of white hair reflecting the light of the rising moon like a novelty lamp. To give the Sovariagn technicians time to recalculate the co-ordinates of the transmission beam without any local inhabitants blundering into it, she ringed the pavilion with an energy field powerful enough to deter wildlife and make any human who got too near feel very queasy. Because the granite bowl was so huge, the pavilion didn't have enough room for courting couples anyway.

Cloval had barely completed the task when she heard footsteps coming down the grand avenue steps. Not waiting to double-check the energy field, the technician ran off into the darkness with a turn of speed that would have confused a swooping owl. Whoever was coming must have seen the flash of her hair and silver suit.

Exhausted and with no idea where she was going, Cloval stopped to listen.

No one was following her.

Although it provided just enough illumination to prevent her blundering into more brambles, this planet's moon continued to take a perverse delight in picking out her silver suit and making her glow like a mirror ball. At least the Monitor had provided all the planet's major dialects which she could plug into her brain's language centre.

As the night air took on a chill edge she was able to think clearly again.

CHAPTER 9

Thumper looked suspiciously at the carrot pie. It seemed to be growing larger and larger the more she and Daffy consumed.

Porky and Pine had left through their flap to do battle with the local hedgehogs over their nightly dish of cat food, so they couldn't be roped in to help demolish it. Tinker and Bonso, a couple of small terriers, had a go at pieces of the crust with all the courage of their breed, and then decided that carrot was not to their taste.

Daffy was just about to wash down her third helping with a glass of stout when a spaniel in the hall started to howl; a sure sign someone was coming to the front door. Knowing she was going to get indigestion whether she moved or not, Daffy pushed herself up and padded out to open it.

Someone was tapping as though unsure how to attract attention even though there was a large doorknocker and illuminated doorbell. Poachers always came to the back, and Daffy didn't expect to see one of them so soon after the last prosecution.

Uncharacteristically, none of the gallant hounds rushed at the door as she opened it and her hand automatically reached down to restrain empty space.

As soon as they saw the visitor, the dogs fled. Animals too old or small to jump obstacles vaulted the full height of the gate to the stairs or tumbled over each other to reach the dining room where Thumper was still pondering the carrot pie.

Daffy had a remarkable capacity to cope with bizarre situations, but what confronted her made her believe that it was an optical illusion brought on by a surfeit of carotene.

But this sweltering alien was real. It had to be from another planet because it was too strange to be even one of Thumper's friends.

Daffy's knees buckled. She crashed to the doormat and

sat gawping at the visitor.

The creature might have passed for half human on a darker night, but the moon was taking perverse delight in highlighting the white hair framing its flattened alien features. The eyes had no whites; they were filled with iridescent hues that suggested they had evolved under a different sun. The tall, wiry frame was tightly clad in a material that gleamed like chrome and various insignia sparkled on her shoulder, belt and collar, the nearest thing to an audition for a Christmas tree Daffy had ever set eyes on.

The alien stumbled inside and pulled the door to behind it.

To Daffy's amazement the alien announced in perfect English, 'Good evening. I hope I have not alarmed you?' She didn't even sound as though she was reading the words from an English phrase book.

Thumper had noticed the strange behaviour of the dogs, heard the dull thud as her aunt hit doormat and the ensuing silence broken by Cloval.

Puzzled, she wandered into the hall.

Thumper's first thought, on seeing the dazzling alien, was to wonder how on earth Daffy could have been expected to cater for a hairy creature that size. The second, that the creature was from another planet.

Thumper hauled Daffy to her feet, neither of them taking their gaze off the interloper.

'It is very warm this evening.' The sweltering Cloval hoped that understatement would soothe their amazement.

'Depends on what you're used to.' Thumper tried to recall the seminar the students at her college had attended to discuss the possibility of first encounter with an alien. They came to a decision about dealing with a situation just like this.

First, you needed to show that you were friendly.

Cloval was familiar with first contact. 'I'm not dangerous.'

There was also a consensus about not showing alarm, however strange the alien.

'I didn't mean to frighten you.'

Then offer some token the extraterrestrial could assess your intentions from.

'Do you like carrot pie?' Thumper had no idea why she asked that. The sight of the alien had wiped every sensible thought from her mind.

Cloval gave herself a moment to try and work out what a carrot was. The language implant wasn't strong on root vegetables. 'That is food?'

'Yes.'

'I would rather have something to drink. I am very thirsty.'

'Milk? Water? Stout? Milk stout?' Daffy babbled.

Cloval wondered what damage her sudden appearance had done to the only chance of persuading someone to help her. 'I have not had anything to drink for some time and feel the heat very much.' Cloval swayed. How long would it take this odd couple to grasp her predicament?

'I'll get some iced water.' Thumper dashed to the kitchen without giving herself time to wonder who was running the risk of contaminating whom.

Daffy regained enough presence of mind to catch Cloval before she crumpled to the floor, and helped her into the living room. The dogs promptly left to cringe somewhere else. It was obvious that under her matted hair, the alien was seriously overheating.

Thumper returned with a jug and glass of iced water. Cloval drank some then splashed the rest on her face and into her hair.

Aunt and niece struggled to think of something rational to say.

'Come far, have you?' Daffy desperately tried not to condescend, but still managed to sound like a primary school teacher. 'Whatever you came in break down, did it?'

Cloval managed to suppress her usually abrasive manner. 'Something like that.' Hopefully the human's patronising manner was due to shock at encountering her on the doorstep. The technician had to concede that her appearance was astounding, even on her own planet. 'I did not arrive in the sort of vehicle you would recognise.'

Thumper was used to the company of Goths, students of quantum mechanics, and ostrich farmers: nothing astounded her for long.

She hauled out the small stool from under the sewing machine and sat beside Cloval's armchair. 'Tell us what happened?'

One of the legs of the stool disintegrated under Thumper's weight before the alien could explain.

'Porky again!' It sounded as though it was a regular occurrence. 'Chews anything if you don't stop him.'

Cloval braced herself not to react. Her automatic response might have been taken as an insult in this strange world, so much odder than she had counted on.

Thumper picked herself up and kicked a battered pouffe over. 'Wonder what would happened to that rodent if he gnawed some wood treated for dry rot?'

'Oh Thumper, really,' admonished her aunt. 'We don't want our guest to think we're cruel, do we.'

'He..? She..?' Thumper stopped. Did aliens have gender? Were sex chromosomes universal? Despite the tight suit and perfect English, it was impossible to judge what sex this one was, let alone how many its species might have had.

The human's ignorance irritated Cloval. Just how exotic did she have to be before they let her explain what had happened? She ran the risk of melting into an embarrassing puddle before they found out how to help. 'You would categorise me as female - a functional, non-breeding female.'

Daffy laughed nervously. 'You speak remarkable English for an... alien.'

'My name is Cloval. You are Aunt Daffy?' It sounded like an accusation. 'And you are Thumper?'

Rightly or wrongly, Daffy detected a dangerous edge in

her tone. 'That's right.' Then she had an uncomfortable thought. 'You haven't been spying on us, have you?'

'Why would I do that? I have had more pressing matters on my mind, like how to survive on this planet.' Before either of them could interrupt with any more inconsequentialities, Cloval went on. 'As you can see, the heat here does not agree with me, and the transmit route I used became unstable before I could return.'

Thumper's only knowledge on the subject of travel was the unreliable condition of her battered Mini. 'Sounds a dangerous way to get about.'

'Only if one forgets to pick up the recall unit which sends you back.'

Thumper inwardly gloated for a few seconds. There was something comforting about highly advanced aliens being just as absent-minded as humans, though Daffy wasn't so sure. That depended on what highly advanced piece of technology they were being absent-minded with. At least Cloval didn't look like Darth Vader... then, what intelligent alien would. And if she was spearheading some invasion of Earth, she would have at least remembered to bring her own ice.

On the other hand, those who appeared benign could often be the most dangerous. She had to be holding something back.

Cloval realised what was going through their minds. 'Being civil does not come naturally to me,' she explained. 'If I were to be myself, I doubt you would be so unperturbed by my presence here - and I need your help.'

Totally missing the veiled threat, Thumper relaxed. 'Well, there you have it! Her only secret weapon is a bad temper. There's nothing very alien about that.'

Though Cloval apparently hadn't plans to exterminate the immediate neighbourhood or metamorphose into something reptilian, doubts still nagged Daffy.

'What sort of alien are you? Why did you want to come here anyway? There must be more interesting planets to visit?'

'Oh, this world was designated when you had more hair than we did. I think your last ice age appealed to the selectors. The climate's certainly changed since then.'

'That's a long while to decide whether you wanted to come?'

'We have to plot well ahead. Takes time to establish a transmit link. Dimensional drift and gravitational factors have to be accounted for. This one should have been easy.'

Daffy was still trying to take in how the Space Shuttle got into orbit. 'What's a transmit link?'

'We don't use spacecraft. All that hardware and time lag; it's clumsy and no good if you want to return to the same point in history when you left it. We leave all that to other planets. They've been trying to crack our technology for aeons. Given the time it took us to perfect the system, we are not going to share it.' Cloval gave Daffy an acidic glance and the multi-coloured eyes iridesced mischievously. 'Invading the worlds of lower life forms isn't part of the agenda.'

Daffy prickled with annoyance. 'I suppose your brain's really the size of a planet but you're in some sort of disguise?'

'Oh don't argue,' scolded Thumper. 'I want to know how they can jump through space without any hardware?'

'So would half the Galaxy,' Cloval told her.

'It's all right. I wouldn't understand. I have enough trouble with the Mini.'

There was no harm in explaining the principal in simple terms. 'We are transmitted from one planet to another instantaneously.'

Thumper's grasp of physics wasn't that basic. 'But even light takes time to travel from one point to another.'

'We do not use electromagnetic waves. We use an elementary particle it will probably take your scientists several more centuries to discover. Controlled successfully, the transmission can be as smooth as sliding down a snow chute.

'What happens if there are any fluctuations?'

'The subject self-combusts and disintegrates.'

Perhaps it didn't sound so much fun after all.

Any technology was gobble-de-gook to Daffy. She had heard of people bursting into flames and had always assumed it was something to do with alcohol.

There was an awkward pause.

Thumper thought it best to come back to the real, albeit rather peculiar, world. 'So what happens now?

'I have calculated the time it will take the portal to become operational again, and safe enough for a technician to be sent through with a recall collar. It will take longer than I can survive in this heat.'

'We'll think of something.'

Daffy refused to be mollified. 'How do we know you aren't using us?'

'Well of course I'm using you. My life depends on it. If you don't trust me, there is something you can do about it.'

'What's that?'

'The other reason I need to hide is because I have been seen.'

'We know,' said Thumper, 'but nobody's been able to find you, including the police dogs.'

Cloval may have been smiling like any human. Because her expression was covered with so much hair it wasn't possible to be sure. 'Small boys and your local law enforcement do not worry me. Someone else has taken the sighting a little more seriously. Even if I don't have a brain the size of a planet, it could still be useful to many agencies which seem to proliferate on this world. We have been monitoring it long enough to know how much humans have invested in weapons technology. I have no wish to become a cog in your barbarous machinery.' Cloval turned to Daffy. 'However much you doubt me, I suspect the misgivings you have about your own ruling hierarchies are far greater.'

Daffy knew that all too well governments unable to deal with climate change would be unlikely to comprehend anything Cloval told them. But there was always a risk of one unscrupulous scientist with the genius to understand just enough.

'What sort of transmission particles do you use then?' Thumper suddenly asked.

'Ones which could be modified for a million murderous purposes. I may only be a technician where I come from; here I could be the answer to a despot's prayer. I don't know who has detected me, and I'm not keen to find out.' Cloval's strange eyes became glazed.

'What's happening to her?'

Daffy wasn't bothered. 'Just dozing off. Not surprised. Even aliens must need sleep.'

CHAPTER 10

After night fell, the deserted country estate where the alien and sinister met was bathed in the moon's silver sheen.

The silent, dark manor house from which all roads and overgrown paths radiated away loomed like a monstrous spider at the centre of its disorganised web. The family's agents regularly inspected the listed building. They supervised essential repairs and sent reports of the work to the ex-pat owners. Otherwise the large house slumbered, hibernating under its blanket of ivy. It was impenetrable to the regular burglar, but there was always someone able to outwit the security alarms and automatic grilles, one who understood that human technology was of little consequence when compared to that of an alien capable of travelling from planet to planet on no more than a quantum anomaly. It was the ideal place for an alien to hide.

Concealed in the portico's shadow, Magin drew a pen from his pocket. With a "click" it sent out a signal that disconnected the security beam on the other side of the door. He switched on the powerful magnet in its cap and drew back the massive bolts. Then all he needed was a bent nail to turn the tumblers of the ancient lock.

For the next two hours the agent silently stalked corridors, searched cupboards and listened for the creaking of floorboards. It was so quiet, he could hear the woodlice.

The rooms were huge and panelled, lit by the moon shining through security grilles over the windows. Even without plush curtains, every inch radiated the aura of ill-gotten wealth from plantation slave labour. Valuable pictures, less expensive to insure than warehouse, still hung on the walls. Even some silver, porcelain and crystal remained in its glass cabinets. No wonder the security was tight enough to deter a professional burglar.

Magin easily broke the security codes of one or two display cases to examine the treasures languishing there, unloved, untouched, and unadmired. So much decorated porcelain, glassware and silver should have been taking pride of place in a museum. An aristocratic family burdened with death duties would have parted with it long ago, but the owners of this manor house owned goldmines and property in Monte Carlo. The estate was merely another resource waiting for a speculator to purchase it for a golf course. Before replacing every item he touched, Magin carefully wiped its surface with his soft handkerchief monogrammed with an ornate M.

After a thorough search of the sculleries, cellars and servants' quarters he found nothing suspicious. That meant that he would have to deal with that prickly young woman possessing more wit and perception than should be allowed in a scruffy student barely out of her teens.

The agent pulled the dust cover from a large wing armchair and sat down to think. It looked as though Magin would have to engage in his favourite pastime, a battle of wits. Not many played that game with him through choice. Only a very brave friend or desperate enemy would try to match his intellect. It would take more than the minds of a million mice to outwit this cat.

Magin leant back, half closed his eyes and fell into a light sleep until the early sunlight patterned the floor.

The water in the downstairs bathroom had not been disconnected and laundered towels were still in an airing cupboard as though waiting for a battalion of servants. Magin freshened his immaculate appearance, careful not to leave any DNA traces. The bathroom mirror was ancient, and had seen the faces of every footman, scullery maid, butler, and cook who had served in the manor house since it was built. A psychic might have detected their presence in the flawed, discoloured glass which held Magin's gaze like cobra about to strike. This was an unfamiliar sensation, not one he wanted again.

Most agents felt like shape-shifters at some time or another. Or perhaps it was that faceless demon which always seemed to be perching on his shoulder, the fear that haunts the hunter who knows too much to fail.

For a second the tall, spare frame shivered. Magin hardened his thoughts and wrestled the apprehension into submission. Failure was not written into his genes. Mortality was a mere inconvenience, and all the attendant emotions peripheral. This was a game he had to win. More than one person's survival depended on it.

CHAPTER 11

Cloval was unaware that she had been asleep and wondered why she wasn't dead of heatstroke. Her hair was wet and silver suit unfastened. A nearby fan was going full blast.

'Feeling better?' Daffy asked.

'I feel dreadful.'

Thumper didn't expect her to be anything else: she was just relieved not to have a dead alien to deal with. 'We reckon we know who the mysterious character spying on us is.'

Cloval woke with a start. 'I wasn't imagining him?'

'That satanic looking man this morning - he was asking if I'd seen anything strange.'

Cloval hadn't yet managed to switch into conciliatory mode. 'So, if you do not trust me, you should turn me over to him.'

Daffy was indignant at the suggestion that she could be that ruthless. 'Good grief, what do you take us for?'

'And I wouldn't be able to stand seeing the smug expression on that man's face,' Thumper added.

She was good at summing people up. That's why she didn't have many friends. It was perversely reassuring that Cloval's bad temper indicated how some things were a Universal constant. Between the sinister stranger and a grouchy alien, Thumper knew which one she preferred. An argumentative pacifist was far more trustworthy than a charming psychopath.

'Why are you so bad-tempered?' Thumper asked without warning.

Cloval wasn't surprised by the question. 'Where I come from, it's the only way to express dissatisfaction.'

'I suppose every species needs to throw the odd tantrum now and then to stimulate evolution.'

Cloval's tone was loaded with self-contempt. 'We're above evolution. Some believe the Sovariagn species are about to ascend into a universally enlightened...'

'Nirvana?' Thumper immediately realised that she shouldn't have ended the sentence.

'Something like that. It's all bunk of course.' Cloval mopped the perspiration from her face.

'Go on then?'

'Promise to hide me.'

'Hide you where?'

'Somewhere as cool as possible.'

'The cellar - but that'd be the first place they'd search.'

'We'll put you in the deep freeze,' announced Daffy.

'You have got to be joking!' protested Thumper.

'No one else can be aware of how much Cloval feels the heat. It would hardly occur to anyone to look for her in there. And she can bolt it from the inside.'

'But she'd be sitting on ice?'

'The freezing points on our planets are different,' explained Cloval. 'To me it would seem like sitting on warm ice.'

It occurred to Thumper that she was suffering from temperature chauvinism, so she relented. 'What will you eat, though?'

'I only require fluid. My body will not need to generate warmth or energy while I'm here. I can go without food for some while. Our species have also developed delicate biologies that can suspend our bowel actions to prevent inconvenience.' The cutting edge returned to Cloval's tone. 'Our species is so pure and proper, senior officials have to wear weighted hems to stop them drifting into the stratosphere.'

'If you were allowed anything worse than a bad temper, I reckon you could be pretty dangerous,' Daffy decided disapprovingly.

'Oh, they thought about that as well,' Cloval ploughed on regardless. 'No one breaks or makes laws any more. It isn't worth it. The punishment for most things is unremitting boredom. Suffering was abolished long ago - for most creatures anyway. The Sovariagn do not have a word for discomfort. That's why no one ever tries to change to the law.'

Despite Daffy's attempts to indicate that she shouldn't ask, Thumper demanded all the same, 'How do you mean?'

Sweltering or not, Cloval's priorities were driven by the inadequacies of her own planet's social system. 'Apparently, aeons ago some saintly twerp offered her life to reform an unjust legal system. This extreme act of piety then became the standard, so changing the law costs the life of anyone who feels strongly enough to do it. The system is so novel many other civilisations with civil disorder problems envy the arrangement. Tyrannies know that not many sensible people feel strongly enough to be carbonised for a just cause and believe that pragmatism is the quality of a superior civilisation. Sovariagn's laws are just good enough to keep most people happy.'

The disgruntled Cloval was too old to qualify for virtuous immolation, though Thumper didn't believe that she would do it for one moment. The young were also excluded because, probably like the old who had nothing to lose, they had a keen sense of injustice. The Sovariagn birth rate was too low to have their offspring sacrificing themselves for causes they would no longer bother about when they reached "maturity". Conformity was a disease of the middle years and most species Cloval's team had observed educated compassion out of their young so efficiently it took them a lifetime to grow it back.

'Can all you travel technicians afford to have such a hard view of the Universe?' asked Daffy.

Cloval didn't regard herself as a hypocrite, just pragmatic. 'The more you know, the harder you become.'

'You're just a cynic. It wouldn't surprise me if someone had thrown a switch to strand you here.'

'The only creatures with that sort of motive are the scouts, and I never noticed one of them about. Dear Monitor Forram would have probably had to pack its lunch before he sent it out anyway. Gossamer-brained fool. He fusses over his creatures like a clucking...'

'Hen?' prompted Thumper.

'Dagglefoot switchcrest. Don't have birds on Sovariagn.'

'Oh.'

Cloval internally relented a little. It was understandable no one else cared that much for the scouts, and that they were treated like machines. They probably didn't feel in the same way as everyone else. None of them looked Sovariagn, so it was difficult to tell. They didn't even resemble each other, just different aliens.

'What will happen when you get back?' asked Thumper.

'Nothing. I'll just be investigated. Some ancient travel technician made a sacrifice to the effect that we should all be a privileged lot.'

'Don't be so flippant,' scolded Daffy. 'Altruism like that is a rare thing - on any planet.'

Cloval didn't have the energy to patronise any more. Humans may have been hypocrites, and totally oblivious of the fact, but were such a wonderful mess, inside and out. Unlike the Sovariagn, whose intestines were even a standard length. At least the elderly could be as rude as they liked. Once past the age of majority they didn't usually have the opportunity to be anything else. Cloval had escaped being sent to manage a park or weave tapestries because she was some sort of genius. The Sovariagn didn't retire because they were never ill. They just dropped dead, preferably when not too many people were watching. Bad manners that. No Sovariagn liked to be reminded of their mortality. And if Cloval did drop dead on her hosts, they could always keep her in the deep freeze until someone came through the transmission portal to collect their troublesome technician.

'If I do die it's probably best you don't feed me to your animals,' the alien suddenly announced, 'Sovariagn flesh is poisonous to most creatures. We managed to evolve without experimenting in cannibalism.'

'Oh really!' protested Daffy. 'As if we would do something like that!'

'There's nothing wrong in being poisonous. Think of all the trouble it could have saved your species.'

'Well, don't you ever... you know?' asked Thumper.

Cloval looked puzzled.

'Bite each other?'

'Bite each other? What for?'

'Well - making love?'

'Biting the person you're making love to sounds just the sort of thing you muddled humans would do. It's not surprising you're so confused if you have to sink your teeth into each other just to conceive.'

'What do the Sovariagn do then?' snapped Daffy. 'Shake hands?'

'Even though your species took so long working out what caused babies, you still managed to overpopulate the planet.' Cloval stretched and yawned.

'That's because we're not poisonous.'

Cloval began to doze. Her lids fluttered then closed over the iridescent eyes.

'Drat, she's going to sleep again.'

'She probably hadn't counted on being argued into a state of exhaustion,' scolded Thumper.

'Well she can't sleep there.' Then Daffy noticed that Thumper was gazing at the travel technician in disbelief. 'What's the matter?'

'Hasn't it registered yet?'

'What?'

'We might be the first humans to encounter an alien.'

'She isn't alien enough for my liking.'

'Aunt Daffy!'

'If the Universe is peopled with species that much like us, I don't hold out much hope for it.'

Thumper cautiously reached out to touch Cloval. 'Do you think I was poisoned when I opened her suit?'

'Of course not, she just said that to shock us.'

'Thank God for that.'

'Better make sure the dogs don't try and take a lump out of her, though.'

There was no need to worry about the dogs worrying Cloval. The mere sight of the alien devastated their canine courage. They weren't even going to defend their pack leader from extraterrestrial attack. The armchair where Cloval had rested became deserted territory for long after she left it. What the threat of porcupine quills could not do to the most determined terrier, her scent achieved absolutely.

CHAPTER 12

The technicians could never get used to seeing the scouts walk into their portal and disappear, sometimes for ever. This made them wonder all the more about Cloval's state of mind as she jumped into the Hell Well to dissolve into a huge Universe and some pinpoint in time and space light years away.

They waited for a signal from the scout they had sent after her.

It never came.

If it hadn't arrived safely they would be out of options. There was no other available for this particular mission. However well trained the scouts who had survived the Hell Well had been, they were alien to every planet except the ones they had been bioengineered to investigate. Some must have been tempted to remain on them. There was no way to tell what became of the ones who did.

Immersed in their own technical babble and on the verge of panic, it was some while before the technicians realised that Monitor Forram was watching them. Of all the scouts his department had provided, the one they had just sent on a perilous rescue mission was special. He had not made the decision to let it go lightly. Monitor Forram was one of the few non-technical officials who had been through the transmission portal and knew the dangers all too well. As he supplied the creatures who were biologically designed solely to satisfy Sovariagn curiosity about the Universe, he had insisted on familiarising himself with the risks they were expected to take. The travel technicians may have thought he was mad, but respected the moral fibre at odds with his benign appearance and manner. And, as long as they did not treat his scouts with contempt, he gave them the deference their peculiar occupation deserved.

As it was obvious the scout's signal was not going to come, it had to be assumed that something was wrong. Perhaps it had been unable to send it and its atoms were now confetti against the backdrop of an alien sky.

As the one responsible for allowing the scout to be transmitted prematurely, Forram reeled slightly. A lifetime of perfecting and befriending the perfect scout only to have it sent into oblivion was too much to take in.

Someone placed a seat behind him before he toppled over.

If the scout had been lost in the transmission stream there was little hope of getting it back. Nothing was ever retrieved from those fluctuations and remained a viable, sane, entity. Worse still, his son had formed an unbreakable bond of friendship with the creature. Forram would not be forgiven.

There had been even stranger fates for those scouts not retrieved. Though it happened long ago, one had become legendary.

An early scout had been lost in the transmission stream after entering the Hell Well. Its atoms had been dispersed before it could reach the planet. The scout's image became scattered over a region of space and remained intermittently visible, so the occupants of the target world took it for a deity. They built a canon of worship about its miraculous arrival and continued to worship it even after the scout's atoms were almost dispersed. Generations later they developed the technology to track the apparition's remaining atoms. So they started a new cult, one dedicated to discovering where the image had come from. When they found out it was merely from a curious planet-bound species with too much technology and intrusive curiosity, it caused everybody involved no end of embarrassment.

Surely this couldn't have happened to Forram's scout, vaporised by the turbulence in the transmission beam? Already faced with an enquiry for Cloval's reckless behaviour, losing that as well would give those who wanted to close the department down too much ammunition.

CHAPTER 13

Thumper lay in bed wondering whether to get up.

Nobody would miss her now the exams were over, and she did need some time to recover from that strange dream about levitating vase lids, sinister strangers, and aliens with iridescent eyes. She reached down to scratch the pricking on her thigh. A porcupine's spines buried themselves in her rump and she leapt out of bed with a yell.

Thumper pulled back the duvet. 'Porky! You brainless rodent! You know you aren't allowed in the beds!'

He had probably been curled up beside her for most of the night and responsible for giving her the nightmare about chromed aliens.

When scolded for that as well, Porky just gazed at her in toothy bewilderment before trotting off downstairs to scavenge vegetables.

Headachy with her rude awakening, Thumper fumbled her dressing gown on and wandered down after the porcupine.

Porky hadn't needed to lift the latch of the gate at the foot of the stairs. It was already open. Any dogs that had ventured onto them fled when they saw her coming and two mongrels sat with an elderly Dalmatian huddled near the front door, more in terror of something inside than desire to go out.

A strange silence pervaded the house which was usually bustling with Daffy and the dogs.

Thumper found her aunt by the open door of the deep freezer, chatting to someone inside it.

It was then she realised that she hadn't been dreaming.

'Are you sure you can sleep on a frozen mattress?' Aunt Daffy was asking.

'It's better than sitting on packages of frozen animal entrails.' Cloval's voice sounded drowsy and a little more alien.

'I'm sorry they bother you. We don't often use the deep

freeze as a guest room. Are you sure you don't want anything to eat?'

'Second rule when visiting other planets; after finding friendly alien - don't touch the food. I just need more sleep.'

'All right.' Daffy closed the door of the deep freeze.

'More sleep?' asked Thumper.

'The Sovariagn apparently don't have days and nights. When they get tired they just sleep for as long as they need.'

'Bet they never need to clock on.'

'Remember to keep the deep freeze light on, won't you Thumper. Cloval can't operate it from the inside. We've decided to switch it on and off three times when we want her to unlock it from the inside.'

'Okay.' Thumper yawned. 'Just as well you had that two-way lock fitted.'

'Well that silly brother of yours nearly froze to death in there, remember. What on earth made him think it was an underground hideaway used by 007?'

'He was going through this phase...'

Her brother never went through a normal adolescence. From the cradle onwards, he just went through "phases". Some bizarre. Some dangerous. Now he was older, they were just tedious. Thumper was glad he no longer bored her with his ventures into pop music or, when he went through his Goth phase, travels with his coffin.

Thumper sat at the table and gazed at the box of cornflakes. 'Do you know what Porky did last night?'

'Got into bed with you?'

'Stupid pincushion.'

The rodent had probably only been looking for a burrow, but Daffy knew better than to try and pick up a porcupine when its mind was set on something.

As Thumper reached for the milk the full weight of the morning bore down on her.

She groaned. 'Oh God - what are we going to do now?'

'Just wait, I suppose. Let's hope Cloval's friends rescue

her before someone comes knocking at the door.'

'I don't think you should have said that.'

'Why not?'

'I can hear someone knocking at the front door.'

'Groceries!' Daffy frantically searched for her purse. Some manic terrier had apparently made off with it. It was always happening. There were still purses buried in the garden. Losing keys was no great deal. Who'd break in with seventeen dogs guarding the property?

'My purse is in the duffle bag on the coat stand. There should be enough in my card account.'

'Right.' Daffy dashed out into the hall.

Through a few token growls, Thumper could hear the movement of crates and cheerful early morning tones of the only deliveryman in the district who dare approach the house without being sure all the dogs were safely inside first. She wondered why Daffy hadn't closed the front door to prevent the dogs bounding after the van. Her head was still too fuddled to draw any conclusions, though.

Daffy came back into the kitchen. 'I owe you fourteen pound sixty and they included a free pineapple yoghurt.'

Thumper wondered to herself whether Cloval would eat pineapple yoghurt? Her species must have eaten something: as it was so cold on her planet, probably totally different plants, tough and deep-rooted.

It was unlikely that the alien was ever constipated.

With unusual intensity for that time of the morning, Daffy began to toss frozen meat into a saucepan to simmer, and collected dog bowls as though unable to remember how many there should have been.

Thumper realised that the hound which usually hurled itself against the door at the smell of food hadn't arrived. 'Where's Wallaby?'

'In the kennels. We promised to keep him there until he's seen to, remember?'

'Yeah, if he jumps over the fence to Fanny Burton's pedigree bitch once more, she threatened to have us prosecuted as a neighbourhood nuisance.'

'Grotesque woman. Never could trust people who tint their hair red or clip poodles.'

Daffy was uncharacteristically on edge about something.

'What is the matter with you?'

'It's probably only my imagination.'

'What is?'

'That tall man in the black frock coat.'

For a moment Thumper thought her aunt was having a flash back to her long lost lover who was believed to have drowned at sea. When in civvies, he used to wear a long black raincoat.

'What about him?'

'He isn't the new vicar of St Anne's.'

Thumper nearly choked on her cornflakes. 'What?'

'He's watching the house. I wouldn't have noticed if the deliveryman hadn't mentioned it... and for a moment he did remind me of...'

'Oh Jesus! I'm not up to facing that creep this early. Do you think he knows?'

'He doesn't have the sort of expression that would give anything away. Best let me do the talking if he does call.'

Thumper detected the "adults know best" in her aunt's tone. 'So what am I liable to tell him?'

'You will argue so much. You might let something slip.'

'Oh this one isn't the sort who would let anyone hang an argument on him. He's really cool. Too cool to be an ordinary copper.'

'What else is he liable to be then?'

'He won't come to the door yet. He just wanted to make sure you saw him first.'

'Why?'

'Something psychological that might have worked on higher intellects. As the only higher intellect around here is fast asleep in the freezer, he's wasting his time.'

Daffy took the groceries into the kitchen. 'I'm going to get dressed.'

An hour later there was still an alien in the deep freezer and sinister man outside looking for her.

CHAPTER 14

The police had given up investigating the mysterious extraterrestrial sighting and gone back to more important duties like monitoring speed traps and rounding up cows straying onto motorways.

However, other agencies had more time to take the preposterous seriously and the military had the resources to discreetly deploy operatives who had read the real X Files.

The sighting of the silver alien could have been just one more leg-pull or a deflated weather balloon. Nothing about it conformed to the usual reports by dog walkers who had watched the other X-Files on TV. No spacecraft, scorched ground, crop circles or dismembered cattle; just the odd glimpse of something tall and silver darting through the bushes of a rundown country estate.

And then there was that suspicious stranger moving about the manor house with impunity. Finding out what department he belonged to might have meant treading on some powerful toes whose owners who had enough influence to shut down any military investigation. Those doves that used to just try and curtail their funding had grown into pterodactyls waiting for the Army dinosaurs to become bogged down by their own ineptitude.

So surveillance needed to be unobtrusive, and by an operative who wouldn't be given a second glance in a supermarket queue, even if she did have a deadly reputation. What Colonel Angela Tovey might do if Magin discovered she was watching him could be a different matter. He wouldn't be the first agent from a secret department to disappear when they were both after the same target.

This plain clothes soldier made the perfect civilian,

having the contours to comfortably conceal a gun. The Colonel had been sent on many missions before, much to the regret of the targets she had been tailing. While the civil authorities preferred to question drug runners when apprehended, and apply for extradition when they left their jurisdiction, Colonel Tovey was more inclined to shoot them and save the state's money.

Despite this, the neat, anonymous-looking woman was not an expert in unarmed combat. Why bother to tangle with someone twice your size when you carried a gun? For some reason, men never expected her to mean it. Because of her reflex for closing arguments by pulling a trigger not many survived to find out how wrong they were. Fortunately she had strict orders to keep away from the alien when she had located it.

Shooting Magin would not have been a good move either. The military would first need to know what agency sent him out before they could conceal his disappearance. If it was only DEFRA investigating entities terrifying cattle it would be very embarrassing all round. He was obviously too well trained to bother being furtive, and that meant he must have had backup.

If he had to vanish from the face of the Earth, it would need to be bones and all.

CHAPTER 15

By midmorning, Thumper was now so curious about the sinister stranger she welcomed the knock on the front door. When it was opened, the dogs skulked away to hide in corners and watch apprehensively.

Thumper had steeled herself to take a hard look at the intimidating man in black. There was still something about him that made her innate boldness quail.

Thumper glowered. 'You still poking around?'

She resented the way his Edwardian style would have been acceptable in a smart nightclub. On anyone else it would have been out of place, but this man wore it with the elegance of a vampire.

The young woman's scrutiny of him almost distracted Magin from the reason why he was there.

This was going to be tougher than he expected.

'May I come in?' He produced a convincing ID which didn't mean a thing to her, and quickly returned it to an inside pocket.

'Dogs may not like it.'

As Magin peered inside the hall, Thumper could hear paws scrabbling to escape.

All he could see were frightened eyes peering from the odd corner. 'They seem subdued. Perhaps there is still something disturbing them.'

'You most probably.'

Daffy descended the stairs to get a closer look at this agent of the Devil or close relative.

'Who is it, Thumper?'

'I didn't catch his name, Auntie. Think we should ask him?'

It was apparent that nothing they did or said was going to deter the man. 'My name is Magin.'

'Oh.' Daffy sounded as though she expected it to be something like that. 'You know who we are, I suppose?'

As Magin nodded, his velvety black fringe parted slightly. This fascinated Thumper's sense of texture and she stared accusingly at it. She had never known hair behave quite like that before. It seemed to have a life all of its own.

Thumper's inconvenient concentration allowed him to discreetly step inside.

'What is it you want, Mr Magin?' asked Daffy.

'I explained to your niece yesterday that I was investigating the sighting of something strange in this area.'

'I realise that the odd person regards us as slightly eccentric, but see no reason for anyone to have contacted some secret agency over the matter. I would like to see your identification please.'

Magin hesitated, more at this homely lady's suddenly forbidding manner than reluctance to produce it. Thumper was surprised as well. She had never seen this side of her aunt's character before.

'If you do not identify yourself this instant I shall phone the police,' Daffy warned.

'Not necessary.' Magin held out the ID card. 'It is unlikely you have seen one of these before.' He tried not to sound patronising. He certainly didn't want to see her reaction to that.

'It looks authentic enough, though I have no way of telling if either of you is genuine. My nephew is the one who believes in secret government agencies. I've only dealt with officialdom where overqualified incompetents have jobs for life. You obviously aren't one of them.'

It sounded like a backhanded compliment, so Magin accepted it as such.

'You had better come into the living room,' Daffy instructed. 'I'm not going to discuss anything on the doormat.'

Thumper nearly gasped in alarm but managed to stop herself in time. How could her aunt allow the agent to sit there with an alien in a deep freeze only a few feet away? She wasn't experienced enough to comprehend their odd interaction.

Magin certainly understood it and was playing the strange game masterfully. 'A very serious situation could be prevented if you are prepared to assist us.'

Daffy said no more until they were in the living room and she was seated comfortably in the armchair Cloval had used the night before.

Magin lowered himself stiffly into the armchair facing Daffy.

'Now tell us about this "situation", Mr Magin,' she said.

Thumper was hoping that the man's guarded conversation was due to Daffy's intimidating manner, yet suspected it had more to do with the cat and mouse game they had decided to play. From where she sat, it was difficult to tell who was prey and who was predator.

'There have been reports of an extraterrestrial roaming this district. If true, there could be a national panic if the wrong person discovered it.'

'So you're here to make sure we can all sleep safely under our beds? Really Mr Magin! Try again.'

There was no surprise in her tone at the revelation so the woman was obviously hiding something.

Magin changed tack. 'I have every reason to believe that you know where this alien is.'

'Go on?'

'It could be extremely dangerous. Even if apparently friendly, it might be carrying infections this planet has no resistance to.'

'Human beings evolved as scavengers, so it's unlikely we would be vulnerable to any exotic, alien bacteria. Our own have a hard enough time trying to kill us off as it is.'

'We cannot take the risk. Human antibiotics would not work on an alien disease.'

'So the military are going to put it under curfew and give it bed and breakfast?' Daffy gave a hard laugh. 'I could well imagine they would like to get their hands on a creature like that.'

Thumper now understood why her aunt was playing the odd game. She was telling the man what he needed to know without admitting to anything.

Magin's response was seamless. 'Indeed they would. Reason alone why you should tell me what you know.'

'I would hardly expect a military investigator to openly declare himself.'

'My severe manner is my nature, not due to military training.'

Having got the military question out of the way, Thumper couldn't stay quiet any longer. 'So?'

'He could be working on his own.'

Magin slowly rose and removed his frock coat. 'Search me if you wish.'

She looked at him in amazement.

'And be careful,' he went on, 'Those things are notoriously difficult to handle. You'd better make sure that the spring is under the right pressure, and it's loaded - just in case you need it in a hurry.'

Daffy was staggered by his powers of observation. 'No, your decades of training were not wasted, Mr Magin. But why put the thought into my head?'

'To prove that you can trust me.'

'Whatever you are, I couldn't shoot an unarmed man.'

'I'm sure you are too much of a lady. Though, in any event, you might find me very difficult to kill.'

'Just you take care of Thumper. She may have the wit of an old woman, but as yet it hasn't managed to grow into her post teenage brain.'

'I promise.'

At last Thumper managed to get her Mini started and she backed it out onto the road.

Magin rose from the settee and for a moment towered over Daffy, glancing back at her with a strange, haunted expression, a mixture of hunter and hunted, as he left.

Despite herself, Daffy went to the stairs as soon as they had gone, removed the walking cane from the umbrella stand and took it into the kitchen. With a great deal of care, she wound in the correct spring pressure and loaded it with a wickedly sharp, solid steel bullet from a tin containing various projectiles which came with the weapon so many years ago. She had often loaded and unloaded it, without touching the gas chamber which she assumed to still be pressurised. She had never fired it because, as Magin had pointed out, she wasn't sure about the damage it could do. Like her deep freezer, the weapon had a murky provenance and it wouldn't have surprised her if the spring gun had been used as a murder weapon at some time or other.

Daffy checked the safety catch, and then placed the gun on a high shelf where no inquisitive dog could trigger it.

Thumper was momentarily distracted by the sight of the firm male body in the immaculate turtle-necked shirt and elegantly flared trousers.

'Do it,' Daffy told Thumper.

The young woman suddenly felt bashful. Rough-and-tumble with students her own age was one thing, pawing a man over twenty years older and a hundred times more sophisticated was quite another.

Daffy had lived long enough to set aside such considerations. 'Get on with it. He's not likely to appreciate an old crone like me molesting him. Throw me his coat.'

Thumper would never get the opportunity to examine a man this classy again. The ones available to her would more likely be laddish, clumsy or as boring as congealed macaroni. She had dreamt of doing something like this in old films. But then, she had been playing the part of Katherine Hepburn. There were no long dead icons to hold her hand and show her how to go about it here.

She started by tentatively searching for any incriminating bulges. There were none. Magin's mature contours were flawless. Then she patted where she dare for hard metal before searching his pockets. The pendant he wore had to be some electronic gadget relaying everything back to a surveillance team deep in the bowels of the earth. Thumper scrutinised the gold ornament with all her instincts for mineral alloys. It was just a pendant.

Riffling through the pockets of his frock coat, all Daffy managed to find was a wallet packed with new bank notes and no credit cards, two pens with no secret compartments, a small torch, a blank notebook, a handkerchief, and bent nail. This lack of technology seemed to upset Daffy more than if she had discovered a Smith and Wesson.

'Where are your keys? Mobile phone? And you have no comb?'

'Are these compulsory?'

'You obviously travelled from somewhere, but have no

train tickets on you, so it's likely you have a car, perhaps even a home. And your hair is immaculately groomed, yet you have no comb?'

'I do not carry tickets of any description because it would be possible for someone less friendly than you to work out where I travelled from. I do not carry car or house keys because neither have locks that are opened by keys. Mobile phones fry the brain, and I have surprisingly well behaved hair.'

'So there is no way we can confirm who you say you are.'

Magin slowly replaced his coat and sat down again.

'Well, you wouldn't have let us search you if you did have something on you we weren't supposed to find,' Thumper blurted out, totally forgetting the mysterious rules of the game Magin and her aunt were playing, and sending Daffy straight down the longest snake on the board.

Magin gratefully accepted the opportunity for his throw of the dice. 'So either way, it is not possible for me to convince you that I have nothing to do with military intelligence?'

Daffy took a deep breath and prepared to start over again.

The agent's dark amber eyes had a disconcertingly mercurial gleam and she hesitated, but it was her turn to throw the dice. 'Assuming the military does have any intelligence, and you do not represent them, what is the nature of the masters you work for? Given your expensive tastes, you're not likely to be the council dog warden checking us out.'

'You flatter me.'

'It wasn't intentional I assure you.'

'The agency I represent is naturally anxious to make contact with any creature from another world, and curious about what it could teach us.'

'Well at least he's not from the tabloids,' interjected Thumper, despite her aunt's disapproving glance.

Despite the interruption, Daffy started to make her laborious way up the next ladder. 'And what should this extraterrestrial visitor be obliged to teach us?'

'However advanced our technology, we are still cosmic midgets, unable to travel beyond our own solar system.'

'Yes we could,' Thumper cut in again. 'If the money was put into that research instead of weapons, the technology could easily be developed.'

'Advanced alien engineering could solve problems that would otherwise take centuries of research.'

'And you think that an alien would tell you about it?'

'Why not?'

The full horror of what her own species could do with one fragment of Cloval's knowledge struck home.

The reason for Daffy's odd game was now obvious.

'Pigs can fly. They take off every five minutes from Luton Airport,' she said.

'Not all scientific developments are engineered by scoundrels. The resources to research them are not restricted to totalitarian governments.'

'And what regime do you represent, Mr Magin?'

'A charitable one.'

'Rubbish! Our knowledge should be acquired by the research of our own scientists. Not coerced from unwilling aliens.'

'Why do you assume this alien to be unwilling?'

'It never came here to shake your manicured hand, did it? I'm sorry, we can't help you.' Daffy got up.

Game over.

Magin rose like an unwinding serpent. Snakes and ladders were perhaps not in his class after all.

With a shudder, Thumper now realised just how dangerous this game was.

'I will give you time to think it over and return this afternoon.'

'Good-bye, Mr Magin.' Daffy returned to her seat and picked up some crocheting.

The agent inclined his head deferentially, even though

she was no longer looking at him, and left.

Thumper followed him to the front door. 'And what if we still can't help you?'

Magin cast her a strange, fearful glance. She briefly found herself looking into the deep well of bizarre possibilities only a person as mature as her aunt could comprehend. That glance was his way of warning her to be careful.

Thumper quickly bounced back down to the safety of her post-adolescent plateau. 'Long walk back to Hades without a car.'

'I'll thumb a lift from Poseidon as soon as I reach deeper water.'

Once Magin was well away, the dogs emerged from their hiding places.

Thumper watched him stride leisurely along the footpath like a potentate about to contemplate his fiefdom. That direction only led to the manor house. Perhaps he was the guest of the resident ghost; he certainly seemed to disappear from sight sooner than he should have. Magin may have been the Devil in disguise but, as a mortal man, he moved like an angel assured of his place on the right hand of God. If it was all an act, he deserved an Oscar for it.

When Thumper went back into the living room Daffy was running her fingers under the seat of the chair Magin had been sitting in to make sure hadn't planted a listening device.

'What do you think?' asked Thumper.

'Strange one, that. Too dangerous not to do something about him.'

'Are you serious? He's seriously weird and scares the living daylights out of me.'

'He'll not harm either of us. All he wants is Cloval.'

'How can you be so sure?'

'He was never trained to kill. His movements are naturally fluid, and that unbending persona is just to intimidate. Had a headmaster just like that. Drill major during the day, Kinky Boots Gloria at a gay club in the evenings, until the police raided the place. Last I heard of him, he was playing the straight Brit for some LA cable channel.'

'Aunt Daffy,' groaned Thumper, 'even if Magin's gay, that doesn't mean he's harmless.'

'Oh, Magin wouldn't risk breaking a fingernail to harm either of us. It's the mind behind those amber eyes that's the real problem. Anyone who carries a blank notebook and not so much as a phone number on him can remember volumes. If he stays around here he'll soon guess where Cloval is.'

'Must have left everything in this wonderful car of his.'

'Perhaps, but it's odd he would try so hard to convince us he never had one?'

'He's probably trendy enough to do without one. You know - trains and taxis.'

'You may be right.' There was a scheming edge to Daffy's tone. 'That could be very useful.'

'What are you plotting?'

'We need to buy time for Cloval's friends to rescue her. How's your car at the moment?'

'Goes most of the while.'

'Well enough to get you to that sculptor friend of yours on the coast?'

'Eccles? I should think so.'

'I want you to post a package same day delivery.'

CHAPTER 16

Two young people gazed at the vista of ice and frost that stretched away to the horizon. The sight could still awe the oldest Sovariagn. They needed no wondrous deities to revere, living on a magical planet filled with creaking glaciers, crackling hoarfrost, and frozen waterfalls.

Like a shimmering dart on the verge of being blasted into space, the towering conductor of the government halls stabbed the brittle blue sky. That hemisphere's power came from the heat of the mantle, which was distributed by the underground generators surrounding the vast metropolis. When there was a surge the occasional spike of electricity cut through the atmosphere from the tip of the flashing steeple.

The icy world of Sovariagn gleamed so much its reflected sunlight illuminated the planet's two moons like huge spotlights in the daylight sky. The roof of the stratosphere was a shell of frozen carbon dioxide crystals, and its seas treacherous with ice floes that crashed together, making seismic detectors ring like bells. The beauty of a once fierce, volcanically unstable world was now benign, captured, calmed, and made to dance to a less cosmic tune.

The Sovariagn laws were ancient. Few ever broke them. Punishments were seldom severe and mere misdemeanours did not carry enough kudos to make it worth while anyway. There was only one way to administer this archaic system of justice. Make it the responsibility of those not yet subject to the law, those who should be above it.

They left it to their children.

Like most other species, the Sovariagn varied in shape, though their inherent delicacy tended towards the slender. This civilisation had an ascetic reputation to live up to and overeating was unheard of. Their diet of plants that had evolved on this freezing world was low in calories. Only those responsible for essential services, burials, maintenance, basic sanitation, and geniuses, were not frowned upon for looking how they chose.

The Sovariagn appearance was ethereal compared to other species who grew their own carapaces or wore boxlike garments to emphasise their contours. There were some exceptions to their natural elegance of course, but these eccentricities were tolerated to prevent visual stagnation.

Fine hair framed the flattened Sovariagn features,

which mirrored emotions, welcome or not. They were expert at reading the moods of others in their expressions. Perhaps the ancient Iglatte race which had evolved below the surface of Sovariagn millennia ago had been too poker-faced for this superior species. They were now all gone and the truth of their disappearance was kept well away from the curious, casual inquirer, embedded in the classified history programs available to the privileged, those above and below the age of majority.

The sun reached its Zenith.

Time for Mital and Alvas to fulfil their weighty commission.

CHAPTER 17

Thumper carefully unpacked the pots, mugs, bowls and dishes from her Mini's boot and daydreamed about the new kiln she would shortly own. Not even the presence of an argumentative alien and sinister secret agent could stop her listing the things she could fire in it.

The shed where Thumper was going to house her potter's wheel and kiln was an extension of the house with a basic damp course, good daylight, electric, and metres of shelving to store work as it dried. It just had to be cleared of the rotten garden tools, sacks of peat, tins of hardened paint and harder paintbrushes, starlings' nests, strawberry netting, tennis racquets, plastic flowerpots, wooden trays, glass in almost whole sheets, hedgehog boxes...

Thumper's reverie suddenly crashed back to earth. She dropped the stoneware dish she was unpacking at the thought of the alien who had taken a wrong turning. It had been one of her best.

Damn that extraterrestrial!

She went back to unpacking the Mini's boot, determined to put the thought of Cloval to the back of her mind by visualising the homes of the nobility further ennobled by her work where the silver salver and Wedgwood once sat, and the Ming vase auctioned so her lotus bowl could unfurl its satin glazed petals on the pedestal instead. Perhaps the great coiled stoneware vase decorated with Veronica's dragons would eventually be promoted from an umbrella stand to guardian of some Grinling Gibbons doorway.

One of the larger and less intelligent dogs, anticipating some tasty morsel, pushed its nose into a mug and got stuck. Thumper swore at the animal and pulled her prize winning glaze free. The ginger mongrel darted off into the small orchard in disgrace.

It was only then that Thumper noticed how quiet it was.

She stopped unpacking to look over the rickety fence to the estate beyond. It was midsummer, yet hardly a bird twittered.

The potter shuddered at the prospect of some alien civilisation light years away desperately trying to reach her corner of the Universe. She couldn't imagine the monstrous dimensions traversed to reach her own planet. Perhaps Cloval deserved more respect, however bad-tempered she was. The fact that the creatures she had told Daffy about could inhabit the sinister cosmic layer that divided her reality from Universal chaos was something only a more experienced mind could deal with. One alien was enough for Thumper's lifetime even if the visitor did speak disconcertingly good English. God only knew what the jabber of a less accommodating extraterrestrial would sound like.

Thumper needed the company of things more mineral to get life back into perspective, not exercises in how to thwart wickedly clever secret agents. Even though she did not like or understand Magin, she had the feeling that something terrible would happen to him if he did fall foul of the aliens. Bizarrely, Aunt Daffy's distraction plan might well save him from a horrible fate.

Thumper tried not to wonder if Cloval had powers

beyond human comprehension and whether she would use them if cornered. But having chosen to help the Sovariagn travel technician, there was no going back.

At last Thumper's pottery was safely stored in the space she had made in the shed, and the items ordered by her customers packed, ready for delivery.

As though on cue, the phone rang.

She dashed in to answer it.

'No Eccles, I wasn't going to stop. I just need to borrow your station wagon for a couple of days. My Mini isn't fast enough for what we want. I'll bring it back and collect mine as soon as I've done... Did you get the gist of Aunt Daffy's letter?... Do you know the place she means?... Great. You don't mind doing that, then?... Thanks a lot. See you tomorrow if everything goes to plan... Cheerio.'

As Thumper replaced the receiver she wondered if Magin would have understood the conversation if he had been listening in. From what she had learnt in the post office, that highly-skilled agent was sitting in the garden of the nearest pub drinking fruit juice and coffee and chatting with Mavis Meredith, the manager of the local supermarket who took her mid-day break there. It was easy to imagine that if he turned on the charm she could have been distracted from her ploughman's lunch. In a perverse way, Thumper was irritated. She would have thought he'd at least put up some pretence of being a diligent and dangerous adversary instead of going to a pub and gossiping with the locals. It hardly seemed the sort of thing he would get up to in his natural habitat - wherever that was. Apart from that, Thumper and Aunt Daffy seemed to be doing all the work.

There was still her duffle bag to be packed before Magin's return. He was bound to tire of the locals' charms and decide to turn up at the least convenient moment.

Before she did anything else, Thumper hastily made a few minor adjustments under the bonnet of her battered Mini, and then sank onto the living room settee to wonder about the wisdom of what Aunt Daffy and she were going to do. Magin might refuse to take the bait and insist on staying where he was. He had enough money on him to lodge at the Toad and Crumpet and watch Daffy's home from the second floor window in comfort.

Thumper was anxious to get the nerve racking business over with.

As though Magin had been reading her thoughts, the doorbell rang.

CHAPTER 18

Alvas and Mital reached the crystal boundary of the mountain garden and once again paused to take in the view below. Their analytical gazes, correct and unsmiling, would have been disconcerting in the young of many other species, but these were two of the adolescents trained to administer Sovariagn law before they reached the age of adult misjudgement. They investigated, judged, and dealt out sentences for laws made so long ago they were deemed beyond improvement. The Sovariagn suffered from optimism, but were too perfect to realise it and remained fixed in that enlightened state like butterflies frozen in ice.

At the base of the lightning tower was the only way to amend a law.

It was a chamber - a death chamber. Anyone believing the law to be wrong was invited to record an amendment in its register. If the complainant did not leave the chamber within moments after doing so, the stored energy of the last energy surge incinerated them.

Their amendment immediately became law.

Very few laws had been altered over the centuries as the chamber had a failsafe system to detect fanatics and complainants with a martyr fixation, and closed the register against them.

This made the short working spans of investigators like Mital and Alvas relatively easy. Once they reached their majority and were old enough to walk into that lightning chamber, they became ordinary citizens. This barrier to immolation applied to young and elderly people alike. Common wisdom had agreed that these were the most idealistic periods of any Sovariagn's life when someone would be more liable to sacrifice themselves for an ideal they would probably lose interest in later (in the case of the young, anyway). So the ones who were comfortable with the law were the only citizens who had the power to change it.

The other category not allowed the privilege of immolation, were scouts, the living tools of the travel technicians that had been created in a test tube.

They had been bioengineered to resemble the inhabitants of planets earmarked for investigation so they would fit into the society of the target world without raising suspicion and were too expensive to lose, even if they had possessed citizens' rights. Their brains were given implants to accelerate their mental and physical capacity. If trapped in a potentially hostile environment they would not have survived without them. A dropped "H" in the wrong place risked as much suspicion as horns or halo in a gathering of atheists.

Given how they were created and the silent hostility they experienced from the average Sovariagn, surprisingly few scouts became defective. They did not have the same rights as sentient beings. Categorising them as biological tools went unchallenged and remained on the statute books.

No one wanted to think about what happened to the defective units. They were just devices weakened by the removal of their implants, without a home planet or right to a dignified death. Once implants had been removed, nothing much was left, only memories. So those who paid the price for Sovariagn cosmic curiosity were confined to the eerie, sky-bound garden Alvas and Mital were visiting, a place where the defective scouts were relatively safe from the gazes of those who found their appearances disturbing.

Mital stopped by a silent scout arranging the pebbles of a border with patient futility. Its arms were shorter than a Sovariagn's, and as the defective unit bent low, she could see the ridges under its overalls where its wings had been amputated. Even if the scout had the strength to fly, the shell of atmosphere a short distance above would have frozen it solid. Only machines plied the skies of this planet.

The gardener nervously looked up at the representatives of the law, still able to recognise the young people who had investigated the catastrophe that had befallen it. The label Defective 20 on its shoulder was now the sum total of its existence.

'How long have you been here?' Mital asked with as much compassion as her weighty vocation would allow.

The strangely bland features flushed underneath matted hair.

Then she remembered that defective units were unable to talk. Their vocal organs were invariably damaged by the removal of the brain implants that cauterised those particular nerves.

'I'm sorry,' Mital apologised with immaculately meaningless manners. She reached down to take the white flower D20 offered. 'Thank you.'

'We shouldn't disturb it. They become even more withdrawn if pestered too much,' Alvas gently reminded her. 'The Park Keeper is the only one who can handle them.'

It was the young people's first close encounter with a scout. The experience was unsettling, like suddenly learning that your favourite group parent is really a holographic projection. Because the scouts were engineered, they possessed few of the characteristics another Sovariagn could recognise. They had no true gender or sense of identity and their accelerated intellects were blank sheets ready for their creators to program. The scouts understood all the Sovariagn languages, yet the one they thought in was alien, spoken on worlds light years away.

Mital and Alvas left D20 for fear of the unit becoming more unreal to their inexperienced preconceptions and interfering with the weighty judgement soon to be placed on their adolescent shoulders.

They strolled up a slope lined with trees that seemed to have more roots than necessary to support their slight trunks.

D20 looked after them with a wistfully wise expression. It had been left to its own devices for longer than usual. The Park Keeper now spent much of her time caring for her latest charge. The wingless angel continued to carefully place the pebbles in a complex pattern as though they could generate a little warmth.

As Mital and Alvas walked higher, crystals in the air clung to their hair and clothes in a thin, glittering crust.

'I remember the old Park Keeper. My tutor brought me here before she passed over. She used to tell stories. The defective scouts were quartered away from the lodge then.' Mital hesitated, trying not to sound apprehensive. 'They say this Park Keeper has a formidable reputation for being outspoken.' She gave a small laugh. 'Seems odd that the only reason I would need to come up here again was to listen to another story.'

Alvas pushed some brittle catkins away before they became entangled in the hair framing his face. 'There is no reason to believe this case will warrant a prosecution. However outspoken, this Park Keeper is past the age of majority. Her views are not relevant, only her statement.'

'Monitor Forram is very important.'

'I've always liked him. He's far too inoffensive to commit any misdemeanour and Monitor Forram's partner, Arbel, is one of the capitol's best surgeons.' Alvas realised that he was in danger of prejudging the issue, but at that moment it was more important to reassure his companion that they had the might of the law behind them. Childhood and all its traumas would have to wait until they were grown up enough to cope with them. New adults took a long time to mature and had to be monitored by their group parents until emotionally comfortable with their new status.

Mital halted as they reached the ridge that overlooked the Park Keeper's lodge.

They gazed down at the large dome. Its pearlised skin shimmered like opal in the bright sunlight, creating a halo in the frozen air. Again the children stood marvelling at the beautiful world that was their home. There was no other like it. Why should they leave it, even if they could? The Sovariagn looked into the Cosmos through the eyes of their scouts. The civilisations they visited were at the other end of a dimensional corridor, so there was no need to penetrate that freezing shell which protected their world. It had been tried: the consequences were horrendous and tachyon technology much safer... unless you were a scout of course.

The Park Keeper was carefully walking a sickly scout round the perimeter of the lodge. It had the hairless sort of face that repelled most Sovariagn and had learnt the habit of turning its pale greyish features away from the gaze of others to avoid disturbing them.

The two young visitors understood that its stooped gait, ugly long fingers and hairless face were no fault of its own, any more than its inability to withstand normal temperatures.

'Is that the scout?' asked Alvas.

Mital tapped her satchel. 'Yes, I have the details in the dossier.'

'I think we should look them over before we go down.' He didn't want to admit he preferred to avoid the defective unit for as long as possible.

'All right. If I remember correctly, there is a small pavilion beyond the rockery. We will not be noticed there.'

The scout was helped back into the lodge by the Park Keeper. Though well past the age of majority, she was jovial, stoutly upright and sported a huge grizzled mane which stood out in every direction

Another defective scout watched D24 take its place by the stove.

As the Park Keeper combed D24's soft, grey hair she noticed the other unit's puzzled expression. 'We're having visitors again. Don't particularly want to see them myself, but there's nothing I can do about it. Monitor Forram decided on this place to avoid unsettling the unit.' She took her jacket off and told D24, 'Don't worry, I'm not going to turn the heat down for them. Do them good to be out of a temperature controlled environment for a while.' The Park Keeper tossed her jacket at its usual hook, missed, then wrapped D24 in blankets until only its beak like nose was visible.

CHAPTER 19

The retreating dogs indicated that Daffy had opened the front door to that sinister character in the black frock coat.

The next minute he was towering above Thumper as she slouched on the settee.

Instead of the dark haze she had seen Magin through before; against the sunlight he had an aura of purple. He had to be an alien as well.

Thumper shook her head. She hadn't had those sort of adolescent delusions since insisting that Winnie-the-Pooh was really a grizzly bear that lived in the rockery.

'I hope I'm not disturbing you?' Though amiable enough, Magin's tone suggested he was bracing himself to be entangled in verbal razor wire.

'No you don't, and yes you are,' Thumper said with all the charm of mongoose hunting snake.

Daffy stepped in before her niece could say something that scuppered her carefully calculated plan. 'I hope you enjoyed your lunch at The Toad and Crumpet?'

For a moment Magin hesitated, as though believing he

had actually been at The Savoy.

'I met Mavis Meredith at the supermarket,' Daffy explained. 'She seemed quite taken with you. Apparently made her late for a meeting.'

A glint of vanity seeped through the stern veneer. 'I'm flattered.'

'It was only with pest control, though. Customer found maggots in the rice. Would've cooked them and not known the difference myself.'

Thumper's face fell as she remembered the vegetable pilaff of last week. 'Aunt Daffy...'

'It's all right. Don't think maggots count as animal protein. Would you like coffee Mr Magin? Or perhaps you've already overdosed on caffeine in The Toad and Crumpet?'

'Thank you.'

'Take a seat,' Daffy told him, hardly giving Thumper time to remove her duffle bag from the settee. 'After I've made a coffee we'll tell you what we've decided.'

Thumper slumped back onto the settee, only to discover that she had managed to land right next to Magin. She carefully edged to the other end of it, hoping he wouldn't notice.

An eyebrow rose quizzically.

'It's more comfortable at the ends,' she lied. 'Porky and Pine sometimes sleep in the middle if they get the chance.'

Magin smiled agreeably. Thumper knew his expression was no indication of what was going through his mind. The thought of being impaled by porcupine quills obviously held no terrors for him.

'You and your aunt like dogs and porcupines?' It could have been small talk or sarcasm. It was impossible to tell.

'We'd both be nervous wrecks if we didn't,' she sniped.

Without Daffy there to disapprove it occurred to Thumper that it was up to her to behave. During her adolescence, her aunt had put up with a lot, but scuppering this plan might have been the last straw so she made an effort to make small talk with this creature who had slithered up through the grating of some secret government agency.

'It started with injured birds, then an old couple over the other side of the village had the know-how and aviaries to keep them, so we swapped them for the stray dogs they had. Porky and Pine arrived in a cardboard box when they were a few days old. Don't know where they came from. They're safe enough from the dogs so we kept them.'

'I've never had a pet,' admitted Magin. 'I would not be able to look after it.'

'What do you do for friends then?'

'I do have some very dear friends,' Magin protested faintly. 'They are more understanding and tolerant than most, I admit. Though I sometimes think they keep me as a pet.'

'Bet that could be pricey for them?'

'I never touch caviar or champagne.'

'Stay out all night?' Despite herself, the conversation had started to nosedive.

'There is nothing outside I really want for. I am very much a cage bird.'

'I can tell by the plumage. Good talker as well.'

'I try to be amenable.'

'I bet you sometimes succeed.'

'You have a very frosty heart considering the amount of insulation surrounding it.'

Thumper didn't usually mind anyone making cracks about her weight. Coming from Magin it brought out the worst in her. 'At least it's in there somewhere. Where do you keep yours, Mr Magin? Do you take it out because it interferes with the cut of your suit?'

Magin was unfazed. 'Oh it's there - feel.' He undid the jewelled fastenings of his coat.

She hesitated. He had to be joking.

'Go ahead, you've already felt in more intimate places than that.'

Thumper tentatively discovered his heart's

whereabouts. 'It's in the wrong place.'

'Refer that to the gene pool I was plucked from.'

'I bet your mother wondered what she'd given birth to.'

'I'll ask her if we ever meet.'

'The stork that brought you must have been blindfolded.'

'That would probably explain why I was "mislaid".'

Thumper groaned. The pun was probably Magin's attempt to come down to her level. 'Who eventually found you then?'

'A flowing-haired paragon who taught me all I know.'

'Didn't she know better than to pick up an egg a long-legged bird "mislaid"? After you hatched she should have had you stuffed and mounted.'

'Kind of you to say that I'm not already.'

The wretched man was actually enjoying this vitriolic exchange and Thumper felt trapped on the verbal roundabout.

She gazed at Magin long and hard. 'Just what are you?'

'An orphan.'

Daffy entered with the coffee and effectively put an end to their irrational conversation. She silently handed them a mug each with no apology for leaving the sugar out of either, and then sat in an armchair.

Over the chipped rim of a pink floral pattern, Daffy gave Magin a look penetrating enough to core apples. This agent did not belong to 99 percent of the human race any more than Thumper and she did. The coincidence was oddly reassuring. This meant she could trust him not to beat about the bush. After learning of his sojourn in The Toad and Crumpet, it was difficult to visualise him laying in wait to garrotte some alien. What emotions he had were safely locked behind the bars of rational thought. With luck, he might even be a little mad underneath the polished veneer. Daffy desperately hoped she was right and that he wasn't dangerous. Despite her antipathy, Thumper seemed to know that. She was too rude and relaxed in Magin's presence to be afraid of him.

'You are a very clever man, Mr Magin. You must know that mere humdrum mortals like us cannot hope to compete.'

Magin raised an eyebrow, half in disappointment. He had been expecting Daffy to reel off a string of clichés too long for a simple-minded giraffe to swallow so he could relaunch into verbal combat. But this wasn't a precocious young adult. The niece may have been able to read people, but the aunt understood the world. She had learnt to be pragmatic through necessity. Why would she bother with well worn metaphors, apology, or evasion?

Daffy decided not to quote Shakespeare or Raymond Chandler. She was bound to get them wrong anyway. 'However...'

'However?'

'We have discussed the matter in depth.'

'In depth?'

'And we still do not trust you.' Magin was about to protest. 'Inasmuch as we have no way of knowing whether you are a military or a civilian agent.' Daffy's tone became icy. 'I have no time for why you want to apprehend this alien.'

Magin's eyes lit up as though a flashlight had passed behind them. 'So you have seen it?'

Daffy was so surprised, she lost momentum. 'Perhaps.'

'What was it like? - Assuming you have seen it of course.'

If her plan were to work there would have been no point in denying it. 'Remarkably like us.'

'How remarkably?'

'Its perceptions and reasoning are frighteningly similar.'

'It couldn't have been an altered human?'

That hadn't crossed Daffy's mind. She was stumped for a moment.

'Why should it be?' Thumper cut in. 'What would be the point? And why would it turn up here?-'

'Thumper!' Daffy snapped. She turned to Magin.

'Bipedalism is probably common throughout the Galaxy. Primates can't have a monopoly.'

'Does play havoc with the back though.' Magin sounded as if gravity were a recent novelty to him.

'You have back trouble?' Daffy couldn't believe that a spine that straight had any kinks in it.

'Just a twinge. Age most probably.'

Thumper had another explanation. 'Peering through too many keyholes.'

'Shut-up Thumper.' Daffy rose and put her mug on the piano so she could look down on Magin. If he had returned her gaze he might have persuaded her that these treacherous waters were actually a humdrum, cushioning ocean.

'It seems to me, that if we help you capture this alien its companions might not be too pleased with us when they come looking for it.'

'We aren't going to harm it.'

'And, if we don't help you find it, we'll no doubt have worse than the likes of you harassing us.'

'The military are bound to find out about it eventually.' Magin wondered if the two women realised that Colonel Tovey was watching his every move. Although they had the neighbourhood spying for them, that agent was better. She could easily have been taken for a lost sales rep, or someone's sister visiting from New Zealand.

'So the civil authorities are going to treat it more gently?' Daffy accused.

'Its knowledge will not be used for military purposes. I will guarantee its safety.'

'Fat lot of use that is when we don't even know who you are.'

'He says he's an orphan,' Thumper announced sarcastically.

'So was my Christopher's bunk mate. He murdered their captain. What's your rank, Mr Magin?'

'I have no rank. I am just a well paid government employee who justifies his wages by doing unarmed verbal combat with suspicious dog owners.'

'I wish I could sum you up as well as my suspicious dogs. A person who never raises their voice in anger is often an immaculate liar.'

Magin leaned on the arm of the settee and rested his chin on his hand as though momentarily foxed. 'So where does this liar go from here?'

'It is possible that we know where this creature went to,' Daffy at last offered. 'If it has any sense, it is unlikely to still be there.'

'Tell me?' The low, softness of his voice belied the menacing demand.

'Us trust you?'

'You have no choice. Someone else is bound to discover it sooner or later.'

'Better it makes the front page of the gutter press than disappears into some subterranean military base,' said Thumper.

'No journalist would dare take that risk. Their xenophobia is only limited to this planet.'

'How far does yours stretch, Mr Magin?'

Magin protested in a tired voice, 'I'm not a fascist. I may have the pangs of middle age, but am not old enough to have been in the SS.'

'The uniform would have suited you.'

'Peaked hats mark the forehead.'

'He's more likely to be one of the demons Buddhists try to recognise in themselves,' decided Daffy. 'The real Mr Magin is probably a beatifically happy bookkeeper with tapioca for a brain.'

It was the agent's turn to resent diversions now he was so near his goal. 'I hate to interrupt these evasions, but this issue is more pressing than my theology. You have obviously worked out some small ploy with which to placate me?'

'We might be prepared to show you where the alien went to?'

'On condition?'

'The only way we can be sure you don't plan some ambush is by taking you there.'

'I see. This is too simple for chess, so it must be poker.'

'Or snakes and ladders.' Thumper gave him an insolent grin.

'I am the snake, of course.'

'All the way down to the ground.'

Daffy sighed. 'Shut-up Thumper.' She turned to Magin. 'If you want to know where it went to, Thumper will have to drive you there.'

Now it was Magin's turn to be suspicious. He scratched his chin. 'How do I know I can trust you?'

'Don't be absurd man. What harm do you think my niece can do to you? I'm taking the risk in letting her go.'

'Why don't you take me?'

'I cannot drive and have fifteen dogs to look after.'

'We can start right away,' Thumper told him as she gnawed at a rapidly disappearing fingernail.

Magin may have been gazing at her with bemusement, or restrained despair. But, as usual, one of his looks was very much like another.

'How long will it take?'

'Day perhaps. We could drive all night.'

'You could drive all night?' He sounded dubious.

The agent rested his head on the back of the settee and stared up at the ceiling's floral relief. Thumper wondered if it was possible that the ornate, entwining roses were having the same effect on him as they had had on her when she was a child. It was easy to lose yourself in the entangled floral swags by staring at them long enough. Magin could never have been a child, though, and was no doubt unravelling the design whilst demolishing their simplistic plan. A man with his brain must have worked out what they were up to: if Thumper could calculate the formulas for craquelure glazes, his mind could grasp their atomic compositions.

Daffy knew that Magin was making a show of thinking the matter over. He could have replied in a split second. It suggested that his answer was going to be more complex than she had counted on.

Magin suddenly let his gaze fall to the embroidered fire screen. 'All right.'

Thumper's jaw dropped. 'All right?'

'I've no doubt that you only put this to me because you knew I couldn't afford to ignore it. I'm beginning to suspect that I'm not as tricky as I thought.'

'You're still very sinister, though,' Thumper consoled him.

'So many years of experience, just to be reassured by amateurs that I'm merely sinister - You are amateurs, aren't you?'

'Mr Magin,' admonished Daffy. 'You have a suspicious mind.'

'I'm sorry, it's just that being thwarted brings out my persecution complex.'

'Well keep it wrapped up when you're with Thumper.'

'Oh, she could never persecute me.'

Daffy wasn't so sure about that. 'And you behave yourself Thumper,' she uncharacteristically snarled.

Her niece shrugged. 'What else?'

'He may be more fragile than he looks.'

'I had the seat belts fixed.'

'You are insured I suppose?' inquired Magin.

'Yes. When I bought the Mini it had this bit of round paper stuck to the windscreen.'

'How did I manage to doubt you.' Magin sat up. 'I assume you are already packed to go?'

Thumper nodded innocently. 'Hadn't you better get your things from wherever you're staying? The Toad and Crumpet isn't it?'

Magin had no intention of telling her. 'No need. I have the money to buy anything I require. But then, you know that, don't you.'

'All right. I'll warm up the Mini's engine.'

'Warm up..?' Magin started, but Thumper had snatched up her duffle bag and bounced out.

CHAPTER 20

D20 was still arranging the pebble border when it heard Monitor Forram's light footsteps. Considering that its perceptions should have been irrevocably dulled with the removal of its implants, it quickly recognised the approach of the high-ranking superior responsible for the scouts.

The slightly built Forram wore a splendid gown, which gleamed through the branches as he approached.

D20 resentfully drank in every detail about the sumptuously clad lace fly and felt intimidated, even though the Monitor's greeting was more gracious than a defective scout should have expected from such an important dignitary.

Monitor Forram's face was not covered with so much hair as others and, though in his middle years, his eyes still sparkled with youthful gentleness. His swift, even movements were never sudden and only emphasised the innate apprehension with which he confronted the world.

The gardener flinched at his approach, so Forram passed on to another defective scout. D13 was trying to drag a bundle of dead shrubs up the slope to the disposal chute. Because of its intimidating size, D13 had never become accustomed to losing its strength. Forram persuaded the mountain of glistening green scales to leave the bundle for the Park Keeper's robot.

Its webbed fingers released the load and the Monitor took the unit's arm to walk it towards the Park Keeper's lodge.

Once over the ridge, he allowed D13 to lumber awkwardly away to its next task. He wondered what thoughts the defective unit nursed about him inside its oval skull, and whether he would have dared be so familiar with the creature if it had possessed a fraction of its original power. Similar apprehensions had lately been pursuing Forram with such frequency he had no need of nightmares.

As ready as he would ever be, he rearranged the folded cloak draped over his arm and went down to the Park Keeper's lodge.

The interior of the dome resembled a segmented fruit scattered with furniture and cushions like so much chaotic seed. It was the most comfortable chamber Forram had ever been in. Unlike the regulated neatness of the homes in the metropolis below, the Park Keeper could allow hers to be as cluttered as she wanted. The defective scouts each kept their segment in whatever order, or disarray, they preferred like so many alien maggots safely closeted away from high-minded Sovariagn consciences. The ceiling was low to accommodate another level for the power generator and storage below. This helped maintain the sudden wall of heat that hit Forram as he entered.

His silent appearance was at odds with the russet coloured furnishings he would have liked nothing more than to merge with.

Looking up from a bowl of broth, the Park Keeper nodded offhandedly. 'They haven't arrived yet.'

'They should be here.' Forram picked his careful way around the disorganized furniture.

'They might have seen me with D24. You know the effect the sight of that one has on people.'

'Is there any change?'

The Park Keeper shrugged. 'How do you expect it to "change" after what was done to it? It doesn't even have an implant left capable of spelling "change".'

'I brought the thermal cloak.' Forram went to the unit sleeping by the stove. He watched it for a few moments then returned to the Park Keeper and sat on some cushions. 'I made D13 leave a bundle of twigs on the lower pathway.'

The Park Keeper wiped the broth from her mane. 'I'll send the robot out.' She tapped a few buttons on a panel. There was a loud creaking and whirring outside as the robot blundered from its garage and off down the garden.

'Have to get its sensors fixed. It nearly mowed down the last investigators to come up here. Just as well the young can move fast. I'll let it get someone important first, though.'

Forram gave her an apprehensive glance.

She laughed. 'Someone more substantial than you. You could be pulverised by the Iglatte ghosts that are supposed to haunt this place. Want some broth?'

'No thank you. I have no appetite.'

'You're not likely to be found guilty of anything, you know. And hasn't Arbel forgiven you? '

'She had no reason to after what I asked of her. I should have allowed my technicians to operate on D24. It was no job for a surgeon dedicated to the well-being of other people. At least, that was the last thing our son declared before refusing to know me.'

'I've got some vegetable cake.'

'I'm not hungry. Your food is too heavy for my digestion.'

'We manage to live off the garden. Don't see why your delicate stomachs can't adapt.'

'The meals you prepare should buttress landslips.'

'They should pile a few bureaucrats against the next one and save everyone a little more grief.'

'Bureaucracy did not destroy D24.'

'Of course it did. Bureaucracy prevents a sane way to change the law. D24s will always be destroyed until this civilisation stops being so bloody virtuous and does away with them.'

Forram looked at her in silence for some time. Though he was used to her novel way of dealing with the flaws in a supposedly flawless civilisation, he was relieved that no one else could hear them.

'I am perhaps a little thirsty.'

'Drink something then.' The Park Keeper thrust a large goblet into his hands. 'You'll be able to manage this. It was imported from that blot of civilization down there.'

'Thank you.' Forram swallowed a deep draught. Though

not strong, his senses needed to be intoxicated. He swayed slightly, and then blurted out the very words he had been fighting to suppress. 'Nothing - nothing but a few anomalies on a brain scan!'

'Don't burst into tears. They could come in at any moment.'

'D24 would have been all right. It was saner than those I have to answer to and they were the ones who wouldn't allow me to make an exception.'

'That's the price for being in charge of the scouts. How many do you have now?'

Forram wasn't to be humoured. 'They have the same perceptions and feelings as we do, and compared to us they are all geniuses.'

'Don't talk like that in front of our visitors. They might think you're going soft in the head.'

'Me talk like that! You're the one who needs to keep her opinions to herself.'

'Why?'

'These young people have the authority to confine troublemakers, you know.'

'What trouble can I cause up here? Anyway, they're more interested in Technician Cloval.'

'Indulging the irrational whim of that precious travel technician is more important than Purgatory for a scout.'

The Park Keeper took the goblet from Forram. 'Don't carry on. If D24 was that much of a genius, it would have known the risks.'

She hesitated. It was a shame it had to be that one though; the only scout to visit the other units she cared for. It seemed to understand them. It was a noble creature in its own way. Forram's son had admired it too much and never saw anything grotesque in D24. He should never have allowed them to be friends. Arbel his partner, only agreed to operate on it for the sake of Delas, in the hope of leaving it with some quality of life. Once a scout's brain scan had so much as a blip on it the unit's implants, the sum total of its power and intellect, had to be removed for fear of it becoming dangerous. Nobody really knew whether that would happen or not, yet how could a Sovariagn psychologist council a creature designed, body and mind, to exist on a different planet? Forram had hit this brick wall many times, but never truly known the unit involved as well as D24.

'What could you have done about it anyway?' the Park Keeper eventually asked. 'Rang the citadel gong?'

'If only I had that sort of courage.'

'What? Incinerate yourself for the sake of a scout?' She smiled wryly. 'I remember that gong being sounded you know.' Forram said nothing so she went on, whether he was listening or not. 'It hadn't been used for so long it had to be tested. You must have heard that old recording?'

Forram shook his head vaguely. He wasn't really interested.

'It's unworldly. It echoes as though the ground is hollow and lingers as if the planet itself was sighing. It's the roar of the dead cursing the living-'

'Please stop!'

'Sorry.'

'I think I will have some broth.'

The Park Keeper quickly filled a bowl with the lumpy stew. 'I suppose you use a spoon?'

'I prefer not to be wearing it when the visitors arrive.'

'Gives you strength, this stuff. I know what some of those virtuous young monsters can be like.'

Forram also knew. They wanted to train Delas, his son. He needed the support of the other group parents to stop them. If they hadn't, the boy would have probably found some way to have his father executed by now.

Forram finished the broth and felt a little better. 'Now I can face mutant monsters from the Hell Well.'

'Don't be surprised if only a couple of children turn up.'

Forram noticed another scout. 'Poor D16. It looks quite ill?'

'It's getting near its time. I keep the unit inside in case it collapses in the garden. I don't like the idea of any creature dying alone.'

'It is very old now.'

'Never been any bother all the time I've been here. Can look at you in a strange way, though.'

The inhabitants of the planet it was designed to scout had a pearly blue expression and there seemed to be reproach in every glance. That was the way the Sovariagn saw them, though. Their expressions probably meant something entirely different.

'I've marked a spot near the other graves,' whispered the Park Keeper. 'If your technicians don't need the body back, I'll bury it there.'

'Then you'll have another ghost to attract the visitors.'

'Visitors? We've managed this long without too many of them.'

The fee for taking care of the defective units paid for the park's maintenance. That and raising medicine plants for chemists made them virtually independent. Though she was obliged to accommodate parties from the metropolis who came up there to gawp.

Forram gave a wry smile. 'Just be thankful I'm not going to be replaced. They might well find another cosy little spot to house the defective units.'

'You sound as though you're going to give up anyway?'

It had crossed Forram's mind. He could tell by Arbel's expression that she thought he was growing madder by the moment. 'My reasoning isn't what it used to be.'

The Park Keeper shook her tousled hair. 'I can't understand what you've got to go insane about?'

Forram had always been detached from the reality basic functionaries, like Park Keepers, had to contend with. Most Sovariagn were too comfortable in their antiseptic compartments after so many generations of genetic correction. Forram just happened to spring from the most genetically corrected stock of all. He had hoped that partnering with a genius like Arbel and carefully selecting their group parents would help their child to be balanced. It hadn't worked. Delas now couldn't stand the sight of him.

'You're enough to get on anyone's nerves,' mumbled the Park Keeper.

'I've had a long while to practise.' Forram loosened his overgown. 'It's hot in here.'

'Take it off then.'

'I want to look reasonably dignified.' Forram flopped back onto the cushions. 'Nudge me when they arrive.'

The Park Keeper grunted and gathered up the bowls.

While Forram slept, she checked the tallies the defective units wore to tell her their whereabouts. They weren't always where they should have been. None of them were clever enough to remove a tally without activating its alarm and so occasionally ran the risk of congregating together in the labyrinth of trees and nurseries in the upper garden. So what? the Park Keeper told herself, there was no harm they could get up to. They never gave her any bother, so why should she report them? Forram's technicians would only put them in isolation if they found out.

D16 started to wander unsurely about the chamber as though trying to join its companions. A small, tidy creature with large intimidating eyes, its face was haggard with age and it had probably lost its memory, the only complex mental activity the technicians allowed the defective units to retain.

The Park Keeper took it some food and made it comfortable near D24. Without knowing why, it ate and stayed where it had been put.

CHAPTER 21

While he listened to Thumper attempting to turn over the engine of her Mini, Magin sat in Daffy's living room and returned his impassive gaze to the ceiling.

'Who was Christopher?'

Daffy didn't want to explain, yet was reluctant to tell

him to mind his own business. 'The patron saint of lost souls.' This time she was sure it was an innocent question. 'He was lost at sea.'

'Lost?'

'You know - "Missing, presumed drowned".'

'But who was he?'

'Why do you need to know?'

'I meant no offence.'

Oddly, Daffy believed him. 'He was my lover, Mr Magin. Though, being a merchant seaman, the affair was erratic. It's probably on file somewhere.'

'So, you have no one now?' Magin asked carefully.

'Are you making an offer?'

'That was also tactless of me.'

'Oh, you probably wouldn't be too bad with central heating, but Thumper was right, you know - you are a weird character, even without the light behind you.'

'You would be even more suspicious if I wasn't.'

'I also prefer my men to be well upholstered and jolly.'

'Now I know I have failed the audition.'

'I doubt if you're used to standing in line for anything unless it was the Guards. Wish I could place your accent though.'

Accent? Magin never realised he had one.

'It's hardly noticeable, but there's a strange inflection in the way you talk,' Daffy explained.

'Dracula's teeth probably interfered with his speech as well.'

'You're no Transylvanian, even if you do dress like a vampire from the sixties. I'm willing to believe you had a mother. I want to know what country she abandoned you in?'

'Not Eastern Europe.'

'I've no doubt the Russians still have their alien hunters and investigations into the paranormal. To any extraterrestrial, it's hardly going to matter who's after them.' Then an odd thought occurred to Daffy. 'Have you ever worked for a paranormal unit?'

'As investigator or investigated?'

'As anything?'

'No, I'm not psychic or ectoplasm.' Magin sighed. 'I am, in fact, probably the least evil thing you can think of.'

'Not a military assassin?'

'No, I commit all my murders in my thoughts.'

'Not in reality?'

'There is a compartment in everyone's mind where deviancy and demolition can be safely confined without offending the rest of humanity. Combat soldiers are merely creatures who have been persuaded to unlock it. I believe in more subtle ways of doing things. I assure you that no harm will come to your niece.'

'She's pretty street wise, but I'd not let her do anything if I thought it was dangerous and, if Thumper doesn't return safely...'

'I believe you would kill me.' Daffy confirmed his suspicion by saying nothing. 'I do not harm people. There is no reason to it.'

'You are still a very dangerous man. There is something of the disillusioned about you. I think that disappointment came to you very early in life, and not because your hamster ran away.'

'Why does my presence bother you so much?'

'I can't make you out.'

'Do you want to?'

'Making people out is usually Thumper's hobby. She found needlepoint too tedious.'

'I see.'

'I'd rather not believe you are dangerous...'

'But?'

'You wouldn't be here if you weren't.'

'One word of warning then...' Magin's voice was soft and totally without menace.

Despite that, Daffy anticipated a threat.

'If you do find you have to kill me, and the only thing you have to hand is that spring gun disguised as a walking cane under the stairs, do it at very close range.'

CHAPTER 22

Magin knew that he was being watched and that Thumper's Mini had been tagged with a tracking device. Daffy may have been wise to the ways of the world, but there were some things she was better off not knowing, especially where the military were concerned.

Colonel Angela Tovey carried a normal enough looking mobile phone, which had a radio link to her HQ on a scrambled carrier wave. She found Magin's apparent lack of any means of communication puzzling and annoying. It meant that he couldn't be tracked by his mobile signal. As for his companion, her phone had been left behind, probably by mistake because she seldom used it. Thumper had such contempt for the sad souls who walked the world with a mobile glued to their ears, hers was rarely used and out of sight.

Colonel Tovey could only assume that Magin would not have left with Thumper had the alien still been in the location, so she quickly powdered her nose, checked her rear mirror and drove after them. As long as Thumper's car remained within a five mile radius, it could easily be tracked.

This young woman and her aunt were taking a desperate risk in collaborating with an agent even military intelligence couldn't identify. Their investigation into what department had sent him had drawn a blank. With no car, phone or credit cards there was no other way of discovering who he was. But then, Magin knew that. He had even used that soft, monogrammed handkerchief to wipe his fingerprints from the cups and glasses he had used at The Toad and Crumpet. He might have left a few in the men's WC, but even the Colonel wasn't brazen enough to retrieve those from a pub's busy toilet. She didn't know whether to admire the man or shoot him.

CHAPTER 23

Daffy resisted the temptation to rouse Cloval for some while. Although doubts about trusting Magin were beginning to nag, she waited a couple of hours before going to the deep freeze.

Cloval had been deep in calculation and wasn't happy at being disturbed. Evidently the Sovariagn need for reassurance was not as pressing as the average human's. Reluctantly she came out into the kitchen.

'I'm not sure this is going to work,' Daffy began to apologise, and then she saw the strange set of crystals that Cloval had been working on. 'What are they?'

'Elementary particle calculators.'

'Oh.'

'They measure time in the transmit tunnels.'

'I thought it didn't exist in them?'

'It doesn't.'

Daffy decided to open a bottle of stout instead of pursuing oxymorons, especially quantum ones. 'Worked anything out?'

'By tomorrow evening the transmit route will be stable enough for someone to bring a recall unit through, though it's more likely they will just send a recall collar. That would be easier. They just need to be sure that the right person will be there to pick it up.'

'It'd work on human biologies?'

'Oh yes. We're very much alike, though they might find our climate on the chilly side.' Cloval realised that Daffy had been working on her own calculations. 'Don't think about it. We'd have no idea what to do with him.'

'I hope Magin believes that you were dropped off by a spaceship anyway. It's unlikely he would have gone chasing off with Thumper if he'd had the slightest suspicion the portal was here.'

Cloval wondered why Magin hadn't stayed where he was to look for evidence of a spacecraft landing. She kept it to herself. Too many milk stouts and Daffy wouldn't be

up to dealing with any eventuality when it really
mattered.

'What's this agent like?' Cloval asked.

'He's the sort of character any sensible government
would send out to make contact with an advanced life
form that landed in Hyde Park. Humans seldom come
better trained and packaged.'

'Can Thumper cope?'

'We're all going to be in deep trouble if she can't.'

Cloval hesitated. 'It may be a glitch in the language
implant, but I didn't like the sound of the way you said
that.'

'He reminded me that I keep a spring gun under the
stairs.'

'You'd shoot him?'

'Probably not.'

'They'll be no need anyway. My technicians are good.
They will re-establish the link in time.'

Daffy wanted to believe her, if only because it was
difficult to describe to an alien the misgivings she had
about her own species.

'If the technicians do what I have calculated, there is a
chance they are sending signals through already,'
explained Cloval.

'How do you mean?'

'They'd be some air disturbance round the portal. It's
all right though, I put a barrier up to deter anyone from
going near it.'

Suddenly everything clicked into place. 'The folly with
that vase - it's your portal, isn't it?'

'Well, yes.' Cloval would have preferred to keep the
information to herself.

Daffy was alarmed.

Magin must have known. The lid of that confounded
vase flew off when Thumper was messing about there. He
must have seen it happen.

When she told Cloval, the travel technician's confidence
was caught by the throat. Suddenly the warm air she had

been gallantly resisting enveloped her. She slumped into a chair like an ancient clothes prop dropping the washing. Then why would he agree to go chasing off with Thumper? He might have liked her company, though by the time he'd taken enough abuse from the young woman he could well change his mind and swoop back on them when the alien thought it was safe enough to leave the house to return to Sovariagn. There was nowhere else to hide: it had only been luck she had found somewhere nearby with friendly locals possessing a deep freeze. Fortunately Cloval wasn't inclined to underestimate Thumper. Although she had a big mouth, even for a human, she was resourceful enough to deal with Magin.

Cloval was suddenly aware of Daffy speculating. 'And if he accidentally got shot...'

'No - Under no circumstances must you shoot him!'

Daffy hadn't really intended to. The thought was just wickedly comforting. 'Why not?'

'Murder is a serious matter. Most Sovariagn have forgotten what it means. I'm surprised it could even cross your mind.'

'For some reason, Magin invited me to shoot him and for some reason I have an irresistible urge to oblige him. Waste of a good brain if I did, I suppose.' Daffy laughed to herself. The man was a strange one. Bit too spooky, even for someone used to Thumper's Goth friends. There was something about him she couldn't quite put her finger on. 'He wasn't wearing a bulletproof vest when we searched him and it would have shown through his coat if he'd had it on later.'

'All the same, don't do it - whatever happens. Would Thumper be able to cope if he suddenly decided to head back here?'

'The worst he could do is take the car and strand her. And that would be a turn up - especially as we thought of it first.'

CHAPTER 24

Forram woke from his fitful slumber to see the stern expressions of Mital and Alvas. They had entered noiselessly, not giving the Park Keeper chance to warn him.

Any hope of looking reasonably dignified now lost, he pulled himself up as though he had already been interrogated and they were ready to pass judgement.

The two young representatives of justice certainly looked the part. Their clothes were immaculately severe, concealing the supple beauty of Sovariagn youth. Their soft thick hair tidily framed their faces and only encroached onto them where Nature had intended it to grow.

For all his splendid apparel, Forram felt dishevelled and disorientated.

D16 looked on with its cloudy blue expression, and D24 went on slumbering. They knew that justice would never visit them.

'I am Mital,' the girl announced, 'My associate is Alvas.' She turned to the Park Keeper. 'Your robot nearly ran us over.'

The Park Keeper was about to make some lame excuse, but didn't get the chance.

'So I have made a requisition for its replacement. It will be removed and dismantled as soon as the order is processed.'

The Park Keeper was open-mouthed for a moment and Forram was unable to stifle an immature giggle.

'Thank you,' the old Sovariagn managed to say, grateful she had chosen to nurse defective scouts instead of children. It was unlikely that these two adolescents could bend their spines sufficiently to sit on the floor cushions. 'Would you like me to bring out some higher seats?'

'No thank you. We have nothing against sitting with you.'

With painfully controlled dignity, the two interrogators

lowered themselves to the cushions, somehow managing to make a small courtroom out of them on the thickly carpeted floor.

Alvas opened his case and arranged a large array of recording crystals in its lid.

Forram was worried. 'How long is this going to take?'

'We naturally want to be thorough. Technician Cloval has given us a full statement. We need to be sure that everything corresponds with what you tell us.'

'Everything?'

'All the data you have had access to, and everything the subjects might have told you.'

'It would be easier if I handed over the department crystals.'

'It is essential that you relate your understanding of the events in your own way.'

Not only was it a minor miracle that the young people's spines managed to bend, their presence should have also brought the lodge's sweltering atmosphere down a few degrees.

'That could take quite a while.'

'We will have an occasional break.' Alvas looked Forram squarely in the eye like a keeper asking the advice of an exhibit in his zoo. 'Just try to think of us as children listening to a story. You do have a son, don't you?'

Forram wasn't too sure he wanted to tell these two frosty younger people about Delas. 'Where shall I start?'

Alvas snapped a crystal into record mode. 'With Technician Cloval. What is your opinion of her?'

Forram sat wide-eyed for a moment as though unsure if he had woken up. These two paragons of the law certainly weren't figments of his imagination and he could not expect any of the facetious assurances adults were so good at.

There was nothing for it but to take a deep breath and explain that she was a brilliant travel technician, yet very stubborn and absent-minded and should have been transferred to a secure retirement facility a long while ago on account of her age. Because her expertise was so exceptional, the travel technicians couldn't afford to part with the bad-tempered genius. Unfortunately Technician Cloval had no time for the scouts Forram supplied, and even less time for him.

He had always been contacted well before a new route was opened so he could prepare the designated scout before it was transmitted to another planet. It was a strict rule that one had to be the first through the transmission portal. Being a strict rule, Cloval revelled in breaking it at every opportunity. It was not only pointless, but dangerous. It took a lifetime to genetically engineer a scout to resemble the inhabitants of an alien planet. While they were able to speak all the major languages of the target world, travel technicians like Cloval needed to have their language implant programmed and activated to be able to understand one at a time. And its effectiveness only lasted for a short while.

Forram broke off as the stony expressions of Mital and Alvas began to unsettle him. These two may have been children, but he doubted that they had ever listened to stories.

'You know all this though?'

'It does not matter. Please carry on.'

Forram's embarrassment turned to discomfort. He was being patronised by someone a fraction of his age and dared not show a flicker of annoyance. He was tempted to seize Alvas's recording crystals and toss them from the park's ridge. Instead, he dutifully went on to explain how Cloval used to dart backwards and forwards through the Hell Well when they were stabilising the transmission signals. Her reckless enthusiasm might have saved some of the time she was convinced she never had enough of, because indenting for the relevant scout from Forram took too long. There was a huge universe out there waiting to be investigated and he refused to release any of his scouts until totally sure they were prepared. However large the universe, the Monitor was more concerned about the stress and risk they were going to be exposed to after a lifetime closeted from everyone else's reality.

Given Cloval's expertise, she should have been safe enough entering the Hell Well - rules or no rules. Even if there were a sudden fluctuation in transmission, the recall unit carried by the traveller would bring them back safely as long as they didn't wander away from the portal area.

Cloval's team had established the link to a target planet they had long been interested in, gathering all the information needed to visit it. The technician had been so impatient to go there she hadn't even bothered to find out what the scout for this planet looked like.

After a lifetime of breaking the rules, the inevitable was bound to happen.

She forgot to pick up the recall unit.

At this point, Forram gave a small giggle. He didn't know why.

'Are you feeling quite well?' asked Mital.

His interrogators must have detected how much he disliked Technician Cloval.

Forram pulled himself together. 'Sorry.

'Would you like a break?' asked Mital.

'It's not necessary.' Forram composed himself and went on. 'So that's how this sorry affair began.'

CHAPTER 25

The old Mini had been chugging along at a steady pace for a good half hour before Thumper decided to take a glance at the tall figure packed incongruously into the low seat beside her. Despite the fact Magin would have been more at home behind the wheel of a Jaguar or Porsche, he still managed to wear an air of urbane forbearance. The gems holding his coat together unblinkingly echoed his gaze of magnanimous bafflement at the creature beside him.

'Why pottery?' he suddenly asked.

Thumper immediately switched into chat mode for fear of saying something rude. 'I like the texture of anything mineral. I knew a potter when I was younger - she's dead now - but she created a craquelure glaze that turned porcelain into pink ice. That started my interest.'

'It did not occur to me that teacups are designed by someone.'

'Most of them aren't. As long as they have a bottom to stop the tea falling out, most potteries will slap a handle on anything.'

'So there is a subject you have some passion about.'

'Bad taste isn't compulsory. I just happen to be particular about the utensils we feed from. You apparently have taste in everything but.'

Magin wasn't sure whether he had just been insulted. 'I never drink from a saucer. Does that count?'

'You're probably too well off to bother. Discernment is now kept alive by the middle classes.'

'Is it my imagination, or are you accusing me of being upper-class?'

'You're never middle class, wherever you come from.'

Magin had noticed the motorway slip roads pass by and that she was driving a very long way round in the same general direction. 'I know it may be futile to ask, but where are we going?'

Thumper was surprised that it had taken him so long to notice. 'Motorway would take us too far out. Car can't do a good enough speed to make it worthwhile.'

Magin nodded benignly and said nothing. Instead, he continued observing Thumper, apparently unaware of how much it distracted her.

Eventually, she could stand the gaze of his amber eyes no longer. 'Something wrong?'

'No, no. I won't engage you in conversation if you'd prefer me not to. These dark, narrow, twisting lanes must need a good deal of concentration.'

'I often come this way.'

'Friends?'

Thumper opened her mouth to answer, but shut it again before she said something stupid.

'I don't want you to think I'm prying,' Magin virtually purred.

'Thought it was your job.'

'I hope I would never be so boorish.' Magin took a quartz egg from the glove compartment and examined it.

'Friend of mine polishes stones.'

'Is this like the glaze your friend created?'

'That's more Artic sunset, though I've never seen one for real.'

Magin returned the egg. 'No, I don't suppose you would have done.'

'You can probably afford to see the aurora borealis and midnight sun.'

'All that solar wind would hardly be good for the complexion.'

Another half an hour passed. Then came the inevitable spluttering from somewhere in the tangled mass under the bonnet.

Magin tried to manufacture plausible surprise. 'Is something wrong?'

'No... no... always does that after a while. Soon gets over it.'

She registered Magin's disbelief and gambled that, on his list of achievements, motor mechanics was some way down. Even so, he seemed unperturbed at the prospect of the vehicle's impending breakdown.

After more spluttering, and some grinding, from the Mini's engine Magin suggested, 'You will try to arrange it so we break down near a hotel of some sort, won't you?'

'I said it's all right.' Thumper knew she could tease the Mini along at a snail's pace for a good while yet. 'It's just overheating.'

'It sounds more like the carbonising of several essential components to me.'

'I'll stop at the next pub and have a look at it if you

like?'

'All right. How far is that?'

Knowing it would be dusk before they reached the one she had in mind, Thumper replied, 'Not far.'

Thumper's timing worked out perfectly. The light of the small hotel shone through the dusk just as the engine's grinding became a death rattle.

She managed to persuade it to crawl into the car park.

The hotel was an eccentric building. It looked as though the owner had halted midway in its adaptation to a Tudor inn and decided to graft on a Swiss chalet. The garden surrounding it was full of roses billowing fragrance into the summer evening air.

Magin unfolded himself from his undignified position in the Mini and got out to stretch his legs. He watched Thumper pull out some totally unsuitable tools from the boot and begin to clatter about inside the bonnet of the car, and then wandered off into the garden to match his height with the delphiniums. Thumper surreptitiously watched Magin from under the bonnet and noticed that he seemed to welcome the approach of night more like a romantic lover than hungry vampire. The hotel's golden Labrador could sense the inferno of thoughts beneath the man's dreamy expression. The old dog had encountered many confusing contradictions in its time - most of them human - but here was a visitor so sophisticated it didn't know whether to whine a greeting or show him its pedigree. Was that profile really once nursed by a loving mother, or sculpted from alabaster? Did those strong sinewy hands ever play conkers and flip cigarette cards across the pavement? Their elegant movements were unlikely to have been wasted on such childlike activities. As Magin removed the seed head of a foxglove and spilt its seeds into his palm, he could have as easily been unloading a gun.

Then the Labrador saw the Yin of Magin's Yang ambling towards them. This was territory it was more familiar with. She was the type to throw sticks for any fit dog and not try to dig up lovingly concealed bones. She also smelt right underneath her lavender soap, plain deodorant and the faint scent of several other dogs. Her aura suggested that she was still wondering why she didn't share the confused social networking sentiments of her own age group. Here was a character who had not forfeited her independence to become "normal". Like many humans and dogs, she probably had reason to feel alienated.

The old Labrador wagged its tail at the approach of another survivor. As though not having seen a dog for years, Thumper made an unnecessary amount of fuss of it.

Magin brushed the foxglove seeds onto the immaculately weeded lawn, almost as if resenting their rapport. 'What would your aunt do if a realistically priced dog licence was ever introduced?'

'Register as a charity and get exemption.' Thumper gave the golden Labrador a parting pat as she reluctantly joined him. 'What are you interested for? Don't tell me you're only the local dog catcher after all?'

'My wages tend to be more erratic. I only get a bonus for missions successfully accomplished.'

'Oh. All right. I'll see to the Mini. You get us a drink while I have another look at the engine.'

Magin thoughtfully contemplated his surroundings. 'Not now. We'll have a meal and book rooms for the night. If it isn't any better behaved in the morning, I'll hire us a real car.'

Thumper was immediately suspicious. 'What're you up to?'

'It would not be wise for you to drive at night on these roads. It will be safer to sleep here and find another car in the morning.'

Thumper had to admit the man was right. He couldn't carry on without her and the more time it took them to reach their destination the better. There was only one more thing to be settled.

'Who's paying?'

'Me of course. Lock up the vehicle. You can donate it to a car crusher later.'

'I thought you were in a hurry?'

'We might as well waste valuable time in comfort than be stranded on some deserted road.'

'All right, if you're sure you want to be seen with me?'

Magin was genuinely puzzled. 'Seen with you?'

'Fodder for people who want to draw the wrong conclusion.'

'I think I had this contest with your aunt. I never won that one either. The thought of my libido being under such close scrutiny is somewhat disconcerting.'

'Oh come on - there's no need to be cute. It doesn't bother either of us what you get up to in your private life.'

'No, I don't suppose it would.'

'Well I'm not going to touch you. I've no idea where you've been.'

'You'd be surprised, very surprised.'

As Thumper collected her duffle bag from the Mini and locked it, Magin noted a car silently pulling into a cul-de-sac further along the road. The LEDs glittering on its dashboard indicated that it was fitted with more equipment than that required for an evening shopping trip.

Thumper flung her duffle bag over her shoulder and Magin followed her into the hotel.

The girl behind the reception desk tried not to show surprise at the arrival of the unlikely couple and was secretly relieved that they didn't want to sleep in the same room. The newly minted notes Magin laid on the counter quickly attracted the attention of the landlord. The unlikely companionship of the tall, elegant gentleman and the short, dumpy bundle of odds and ends was politely accepted as normal for that neck of the woods and they were escorted to rooms overlooking the garden.

CHAPTER 26

There was a sudden movement near the stove.

D16 had toppled over, stone dead.

'Stop the recording,' Mital told Alvas.

The Park Keeper quickly went to the scout.

She checked D16's alien body for signs of life. 'Can never get used to where your lot put its heart.'

Forram joined her. 'D16 has passed. Probably didn't know anything about it.'

Then he noticed D24. For one horrible second he realised that it had been taking everything in. A small glimmer of light in those once luminous eyes opened up a chink into its soul. Forram was amazed that a defective scout could still retain such sentient sensibilities.

It was a terrifying prospect.

'How soon can we move D16?' he asked the Park Keeper.

'I'll put it in the anteroom for now. Tell your technicians they can come up and collect the unit when they want.' With very little effort the Park Keeper bundled the dead scout into her arms and carried it out of the lodge chamber.

Forram sat foolishly by D24 as though he had just lost a favourite pet.

Alvas didn't understand the emotional undercurrents flowing through the adults' thoughts, but knew they had to be respected. 'Perhaps we should have a break now.'

'The heat in here is somewhat oppressive, and there will be a first sun eclipse by the second moon in a short while,' added Mital. 'That should make things a little cooler. Won't you come with us and watch it, Monitor Forram?'

Forram knew he was being patronised. He didn't care.

'I've seen hundreds already,' he answered vaguely.

'I meant, it might help if you were to come outside for a while,' she explained patiently, unaware of the depths adult emotions could plunge to. 'I'm sure the Park Keeper can contact your technicians and deal with D16 without your assistance.'

'Yes, she probably can.' Forram rearranged the thermal cloak over D24. 'He was one of the best. And they do feel, you know.'

Extolling the virtues of mere scouts verged on the illegal, even by Monitor Forram. If those units were proved as sentient as the average Sovariagn, they could claim the same rights. The thought of the alien creatures mingling freely with the population didn't bear thinking about.

'Perhaps we should reconsider this conversation,' Mital suggested firmly.

'When they finally remove that tourniquet holding back your emotions you'll see what I mean.' Forram's tone was uncharacteristically acidic.

'We are not ashamed of our vocation, Monitor,' Alvas reminded him frostily.

Forram smiled. If was obvious that the boy had no idea what he was talking about. He only knew that the law should be totally impartial. If those administering it started to develop feelings, the lightning chamber would never be able to cope with the resulting ash. That hemisphere's generators would have to double their output to incinerate all those queuing to change the law. And after all the propaganda the Sovariagn had churned out to convince other civilisations how perfect they were, they would have to conclude that the consequence of reaching such a pinnacle was mass suicide.

'Don't you two find perfection boring?' Forram's tone didn't suggest it was a question.

Mital felt the situation slipping out of her control. She expected defiance from the perpetrators of real crimes, not senior officials with Forram's responsibility. Perhaps the behaviour profile was right and he was losing his sanity after all. She didn't have access to the manual for that.

'Please come outside with us, Monitor Forram. You will feel better away from the heat.'

'Yes,' Forram studied his fine fingers, 'I am mad aren't I. My son should have my genes erased. They'll never give him a permit to breed otherwise.'

'There is no record of any mental imbalance in your ancestry.'

'It must be something else then.'

Mital suddenly had an insight worthy of an adult. 'Conscience, perhaps?'

Forram turned on her. 'What would you know about conscience?'

At last she understood. 'You were fond of D24?'

Forram gazed at the defective unit for a moment as though furious with it. 'I should have let it die. That's what it wanted.'

'You would have forfeited your position for such an act.'

'Better than being pinned between guilt and duty.'

Forram then realised that Mital was trying to offer him a way out. The investigators were obliged to report every aspect of their interviews and he hadn't given her much room for diplomacy. Alvas still wore an expression of severe disapproval and would have definitely reported every seditious word.

Forram rose. 'Let's go and watch the Cosmos cavort then.'

When the Park Keeper returned she found herself alone with D24. The defective scout had fallen asleep. It would often drop in and out of fitful dreams as though perpetually toppling from some peak, never reaching the ground. She examined the scar on its forehead where one of its brain implants had been removed. It was inflamed, so she applied some salve to the wound. The operation had virtually destroyed the scout's immune systems.

D24 eyes suddenly flashed open and it looked at her like a hunted animal. There was something inexplicably elegant about its alienness. It was hardly surprising that the soft-centred Forram was having a breakdown. He was responsible for what had happened to it.

She felt D24 gently clasp her hand. Its perceptions

were still lucid enough to understand the emotions it aroused in others.

'There's nothing to be afraid of here,' she told it. 'No technicians or dragons.' But the Park Keeper knew it could have fought off an army if it hadn't been robbed of its intellect and strength.

The Park Keeper made D24 a warm drink. There was always something clutched in one of its hands and it wouldn't take the container with the other so she held it to its mouth.

When it had drunk, she let it slip back into its fitful dreams.

CHAPTER 27

There were a few customers in the hotel's restaurant and saloon. The decor was padded and rustic as though some of the regulars were prone to violent outbursts. Fortunately Thumper couldn't smell leather upholstery, otherwise she would have insisted eating outside with the settling greenfly and mating crane flies. Magin would have probably joined her just to see how vegan she really was and whether she was prepared to swot a moth.

The odd couple were shown to a secluded window table with romantic dim lighting. Thumper would have much rather been within reach of the ancient jukebox. Magin seemed happy enough with the arrangement and, as he was paying, she didn't protest. At least she only had to look at him across the table in subdued light. A vase of roses helped to break up his severe contours.

The window beside them was open to the still evening air and light of the full moon. Magin occasionally cast a bemused glance at it. Thumper hoped that the only effect it was having on him was aesthetic.

Having examined the menu and discovered nothing interesting or vegetarian enough to go with chips, Thumper decided on the cheese salad with pickles. She fully expected Magin to show her up by ordering something more exotic. After glancing through the menu, he handed it back to the waiter and ordered the same. He didn't even look at the wine list and ordered fruit juice for both of them.

Dim light or not, Thumper's piqued expression was obvious.

Magin smiled. 'No brown ale. You don't want to sleep too well tonight, do you?'

'The salad will probably keep me awake anyway.' The man was so full of contradictions, Thumper wondered if she would ever make him out. 'Why didn't you order what you wanted instead of having the same as me?'

'I trust your judgement.' He seemed to take pleasure in seeing the contempt cross Thumper's expression. 'You could be very attractive if you didn't make those faces, you know.'

'I'm not arguing with you.' There couldn't have been any other reason for the comment.

'Though I don't suppose you would see the point in being alluring while with me,' he added.

'Well I'm not going to get close enough to find out if you wear woman repellent as aftershave.'

'Why should I? I never shave.'

'Liar. Nature never designed those sideboards.'

'What hair that grows on my chin can be steamed off over my morning coffee.'

'I'm still not going to touch your face to prove you a liar. Stop arsing about. People're watching.'

'Now who's ashamed of being seen with whom?' Magin laughed in a way that suggested he might have once been a schoolboy, even if never an infant.

'Where were you trained?'

'Oh, I went to the best obedience classes. Why do you ask?'

'It had to be RADA.'

'Really?'

'You haven't stopped acting for one minute.'

'You may not prefer the raw me.'

'There's nothing half-baked about you. Overdone, if anything.' Thumper was sure that it was impossible to provoke him, but nevertheless kept trying. 'You're probably from some East European nobility with its own plasma bank.'

But he wasn't biting. 'I'm more mongrel than you think.'

Thumper glowered at Magin in frustration. 'You're actually enjoying this, aren't you?'

'With such congenial company, why shouldn't I enjoy my work?'

'Not the sort of work you do. Not if you were normal.'

'What am I supposed to do when I run out of spiders to pull the legs off?'

'You could always hunt down some war criminal and use his pelt to carpet your lair instead.'

'And hide the natural beauty of the obsidian floor?'

'You live in a volcano?'

'Oh yes.' He smiled mysteriously. 'At the top of a beautifully steaming fumarole.'

'You're weird.'

'Somebody has to be.'

Knowing she could never win this verbal combat, Thumper gave up and decided to play along. 'How is this wonderful apartment furnished then?'

'You wouldn't approve. Instead of the disintegrating doors and rusty bolts securing your home, mine has an atmosphere lock to keep in the heat. There are no curtains because I have no neighbours. The swimming pool is covered by a domed glass ceiling through which I can watch the sky. There is only one thing missing.'

'What's that?'

Magin lightly touched the petal of a rose. 'They still have their natural perfume.'

Until then, Thumper had only regarded the vase of flowers as a convenient barrier between them. 'So what sort of perfume should they have?'

Magin looked at Thumper with dark disapproval. 'You are surrounded by so much beauty, yet treat it with such contempt.'

This reminded Thumper who he really was. 'I don't go around hunting poor aliens so they can be tormented into doing what the scum of this planet want,' she hissed.

'Quiet! Don't mention that in here.'

She was puzzled by the sudden change in him. 'Just who are you afraid of? There's a lot more to this than tracking down someone who has probably just pulled off some clever hoax.'

'You believe this to be a hoax?'

'Could be. How would I know one from the real thing?'

Magin's expression became fixed on the roses as though they were a point in the distance. It was then Thumper could see the deep terror behind the amber eyes.

'This is life or death for you, isn't it? I don't understand how, though?'

'If I could not convince you of anything before, it is unlikely you would believe me now.'

'Convince me of anything? You talk in riddles most of the time. I wouldn't be surprised if your chromosomes were tied in knots as well.'

'There is no reason why you should share the dangers of my profession. Demanding explanations of me can only run that risk.'

'So I've no way of knowing when you tell the truth?'

'It's safest that way.'

Thumper sighed. 'All right. Let's talk about something else.'

Magin gratefully accepted the chance. 'Why are you called Thumper?'

'A rabbit.'

Magin raised a quizzical eyebrow.

'Some years ago I used to look like a cartoon rabbit.'

'Your aunt has a far prettier name I think.'

'Prettier?'

'Yes. Daffodil.'

'Daffy Duck.'

The waiter brought their salads and the conversation trailed off.

Magin didn't eat as though he had an appetite, while Thumper packed away her meal and was ready for cream cakes afterwards. Magin doubted that even his disconcerting gaze could have distracted her from the serious business of feeding. He leaned back to gaze out of the window at the pearly moon and listen to the song of a blackbird. For a moment all was well with the world. Then he saw the shadow of someone lurking beneath the bowers of philadelphus.

'It's a beautiful evening,' he mused, half to himself and half to the bowers of wisteria cascading close to the window.

Still eating and gulping down fruit juice, Thumper watched Magin's satanically sparkling eyes reflect the moon's rays. She marvelled at the unlikely rapport he had with a summer evening she accepted as relatively normal.

'Why not go for a walk?' she suggested.

Hardly were the words out of her mouth than Thumper wanted to bite her tongue. The last thing she needed was to have Magin out of her sight for long.

'I'll come with you,' she added. It would mean indigestion, but she had no choice.

And, of course, he just had to take her up on the idea.

Magin settled the bill and waited outside while Thumper collected a light jacket.

His phantom still watching, he was careful to avoid letting her know that he was aware of her presence. The time wasn't quite right. Instead, he decided on a futile exercise to test his pursuer's resolve.

Thumper wouldn't have been impressed to know that she was being used as an excuse to decoy yet another secret agent.

After forty minutes of trying to match Magin's long stride, she had to admit that keeping an eye on him was more trouble than it was worth. And what could he get up to while she was the only one who knew where they were going?

They came to a converted windmill, the slats of its sails silver in the moonlight like a mysterious midnight timepiece. Thumper insisted they turn back. She pretended that she couldn't remember the way in the fading light, knowing he wouldn't allow her to return by herself. Though reluctant to admit it, she trusted him more than anyone who might have been lurking in the bushes.

So Magin escorted her back to the hotel.

They were within yards of the drive when the agent suddenly stopped dead in his tracks.

'Those shells could have been polished in the turbulence of a thunderstorm and fallen as pink hailstones.'

'Eh?' Thumper had totally forgotten what she was wearing and thought it was some strange metaphor for another aspect of Nature's beauty. 'What shells?'

'Your necklace.'

'Oh those.' He was talking about the shells Mrs Knight had given her. 'These are cowries. Why?'

'They are a strange colour, but very attractive.' Then he walked on as suddenly as he had stopped.

Cowrie shells were probably attractive in their own way, though nothing to make a big production over.

'Colour? You can't see their real colour in the moonlight.'

'I have a good memory.'

His odd behaviour unsettled Thumper just as she thought she was solving the Rubik cube of this tricky character. 'Yeah, well, some people prefer gold, don't they.'

Magin realised she was referring to the pendant he wore.

'Gold can be chased into any form you like. Those shells have slowly evolved over aeons with this planet.'

'You a member of a mollusc appreciation society then?'

'I appreciate everything. Even you.'

As he smiled, his eyes glittered mischievously. To distract Thumper from thinking up another volley of invective, he gave a polite yawn. 'Aren't you tired?'

This made Thumper yawn despite herself. 'Yeah, looks as though you won't need to count sheep either.'

'Enumerating beasts being brought to production slaughter is the last thing that would soothe my thoughts.'

He was obviously taking the rise again.

Thumper at last admitted she was too tired to answer back and went into the hotel.

She was glad to leave Magin in reception and not have to bother with him any more. It wasn't difficult to sleep, despite the strangeness of her surroundings and a nagging thought telling her that she should have been more worried about what he was up to.

CHAPTER 28

Alvas, Mital and Forram stood on the summit of the mountain garden and watched the moon and suns perform their slow dance in the sky. The corona of the first white star crept behind the moon, which was almost half the mass of Sovariagn's main world. The planet could afford to have a companion of that dimension because there was another moon equal in size on its other side, locking the system into a stable orbit. Their gravitational pull had given Sovariagn a peculiar ovate shape with permanently raised oceans.

The Sovariagn system might have seemed too cluttered for most terrestrial life forms who only had one sun and a single companion to balance their world's rotations. With so many suns and moons the arrangement should have been impossible but theirs' was a one in a billion system with the right balance of gravitational attraction, star density, and correct distances to support life. The frequent beautiful eclipses when the massive moons obscured the large white sun and other distant orange sun became the envy of many other civilisations.

However glorious and unique to the rest of the Cosmos, seeing something on a regular basis could reduce it to the mundane in the eye of the beholder, even the ascetic, sensitive Forram. He dutifully watched as the dominant sun's rays receded and the small companion star bathed Sovariagn in pastel radiance while his heart sank because he could no longer appreciate it. It was like having a spotlight dimmed so the details of everything it had dazzled were mysteriously revealed, making the flowers in the frosty garden below gleam magically like dancers changing tempo.

The gentle starlight reminded Forram of the times he used to stand on the roof garden of their home with Arbel and their son. Then it had been enchanting. Now confused emotions clouded everything, even the exquisite panoramas relayed back from other worlds by the scouts that at one time had given his life purpose. Now incredible beauty had been dimmed by the destruction of one of the very tools that had enabled everyone to see them. He could no longer accept that such splendour should have such an unbearably high price. Losing the respect of a child and causing so much grief to a chosen partner was not worth all the scenic wonders in the Universe.

Forram had once believed that the Sovariagn way of life was perfect, as though their species had transcended the need for pain. No demons could have blemished those pure skies. Now everything was seen through leaden clouds of guilt.

The massive domes covering the continent's energy complex pulsed luminously in the dim light. They rippled with movement as though the heart of the planet was beating. The electrical discharges, invisible in normal sunlight, were threadlike fireworks embroidering the backdrop of the deep red sky.

Forram sighed. The ability to wonder at the magically dancing light had gone forever.

The flower D20 had given Mital began to sparkle on her overgown. Everything in the garden leapt back into luminous life with the reappearance of the white sun.

Forram found the reintroduction to harsh reality too sudden.

He broke away from his companions and headed back to the Park Keeper's lodge without stopping to see if they were following. Unprepared for the sudden heat, he peeled off his dignitary's overgown and tossed it aside like a reptile sloughing its repellent skin. The plain white shift he wore beneath it gave him an incongruous air of piety that was at odds with his turbulent thoughts.

The Park Keeper understood the trauma that D16's death had triggered in Forram and said nothing. The arbiters of justice probably thought he was unbalanced already. It wouldn't take much to tip him over the edge. Hopefully not from a high ridge, which would only mean another mess to clear up.

CHAPTER 29

Once out of everyone's inquisitive gaze Magin stole silently from the hotel.

That car was still parked in the cul-de-sac opposite and there was no sign of its owner. An accomplished agent would have known how to spy in comfort so they had probably left the shelter of the philadelphus to watch the hotel from a comfortable seat. Magin should have felt flattered that he was worth the bother of a senior operative, though at that moment it was rather inconvenient. He had things to do and needed to lose her for a couple of hours.

Magin strode off into the surrounding countryside like a night stalking tiger. There was no urgency in his pace as he breathed in night's pervasive perfumes and watched the bright moon enamel the overhead branches. From the top of a hill crowded with beech and hazel he gazed out at the grey patchwork landscape below. In the moonlight it lay like a shimmering garment tossed aside by Titania.

Magin started down into the warm embrace of zephyrs being channelled through the valley where a canal flowed on its sluggish way.

Time to lose his shadow.

Once on the towpath, he resisted the seductive caress of the night air and began to noiselessly run - fast.

After several miles he paused to listen. He heard nothing but the scampering of rodents being hunted by owls and the hideous call of a vixen in heat.

It was nearly three o'clock.

Magin would have started to run again, but saw a light in the porch of a lock keeper's lodge. In a nearby compost heap a hedgehog was happily crunching beetles.

He took his bearings once more and was about to sprint away when a low voice in the lodge's porch disturbed the still night air, 'Too warm to sleep, isn't it.'

If the agent had only been a humdrum mortal he would have stepped back in surprise and toppled into the canal. He skilfully re-pivoted his balance and turned.

'You startled me.'

'I'm sorry,' the old woman apologised. 'It's not often I see people this time of night.' As he came to the lodge's front gate she tied her dressing gown to cover a cotton nightdress.

'Are you a stargazer?' asked Magin.

'No.' She chuckled. 'Insomniac. I count shooting stars, though it's never helped me to get to sleep yet.' Then she noticed how immaculately dressed he was. 'Been to a wedding?'

Magin smiled. 'I have an audience with Queen Mab, to see if she can handle a rebirth.'

The old woman's face lit up. 'You're a poet,' she decided as though that explained everything. 'You mind the water, though. Young fellow taking a midnight stroll - just

111

like you - fell in and drowned.' She pointed to a plaque on the lock wall marking the spot. 'It was about that time I found I couldn't sleep. I sometimes wonder if I don't sit here half the night just waiting for another soul to cast themselves into a watery grave.'

'I'm sure I could find somewhere more adventurous to die.'

'I think you could too. Ever been up in a space shuttle?'

'I prefer to ride on the tails of comets.'

She took his hand. 'Let me see your palm.'

Magin briefly opened it to the moonlight.

The old woman looked puzzled.

Magin closed his fingers. 'I had an accident. I reached out to pat the backside of destiny, so she made gibberish of my life lines.'

A strangely concerned expression crossed the woman's face. 'No. You may have reached for her rump, but she left the impression of her face there.' She clasped his hand. 'Why are you walking the night?'

'When the sun's light fades, everything becomes a little more plausible. I can briefly believe I have a monopoly of the world's attention. When the ants cease to swarm, the spider becomes monarch.'

She allowed him to retract his hand. 'Perhaps you're more than a mere poet after all. Whether you're up to good, or mischief, go safely.'

Magin gave a silent half bow and passed down by the lock gates into the glittering night.

Once out of the old woman's view, he began to noiselessly run once again.

CHAPTER 30

Colonel Angela Tovey limped back to her car, cursing herself for believing trainers would have ruined the understated front she had chosen as her disguise. The agent she was chasing was no ordinary mortal. She had been on her share of assault courses and manoeuvres; despite that, keeping up with Magin was impossible. But he was the only one who could lead her to that alien.

Colonel Tovey checked in with her HQ. Their surveillance of the area where the alien had been sighted had been expanded, and still turning up nothing apart from two poachers, several courting couples, and a sighting of something feline and unnaturally large. There were no readings of atmospheric disturbance or high levels of radiation. If this alien was real, it had to be miles out of the area, having bounced away on a pogo stick for all they could tell.

Then Colonel Tovey did something only an agent of supreme confidence would have risked. She took a key from her shoulder bag, crossed the road and went into the hotel where she had booked a room across the corridor from her quarry.

CHAPTER 31

It was not until the morning light started to leak through the curtains, that Thumper realised she had been lulled into a false state of security: there was something in Magin's manner that would have broken the resolve of the most determined person. It hadn't taken long with her. Idealistic intentions were not enough.

The girl who had been at the reception desk knocked and entered with a tray.

Thumper tumbled out of bed.

'Gentleman sent you some breakfast up, Miss,' she announced cheerfully.

Her head still full of the cobwebs Magin had spun, Thumper asked, 'What time is it?'

"Bout six thirty. Beautiful morning too.'

Thumper threw the curtains open and looked down into the garden. 'Good God!'

'Been out there since I was up. Probably all night.'

'All night?'

'He never slept in his bed. Seemed he preferred to sit in the garden.' Then the girl realised that the relationship between Thumper and Magin was far from close and somewhat aggravated. 'Odd sort, isn't he?'

'Yeah. Odder than either of us'll ever guess. Thanks for the tray.'

'See you later.' The girl bustled out to serve the "businesswoman" with blisters in the room opposite.

Thumper continued to watch Magin.

He was standing by a bush of the rambling roses that had been cut for the dinner table the night before, his gaze scanning the clear sky as though trying to take in the flight path of every swift scything through it.

He would have continued to gaze at the birds if the hotel's old Labrador hadn't waddled up to him. It stood expectantly by his side for a few moments, waiting for him to notice it. Failing to attract his attention, it licked the back of his hand. Magin smiled and stooped to make a fuss of the animal as though it was some rare, exotic creature on the verge of extinction. Thumper wondered whether he would have been so indulgent or even let on that he could allow dogs to like him had he known she was watching.

Thumper gulped down her breakfast. The thought that a cold-blooded secret agent could also be an animal lover almost gave her indigestion. Where could he have got to during the night, though? To hire another car perhaps? There were no new additions in the car park. He might have been contacting his department from a public telephone. Someone who took the precaution of not carrying a mobile would have hardly run the risk of being overheard through the hotel's switchboard.

At least her old Mini was still on her side. Eccles needed plenty of time to deal with the package she had posted the day before. A quick flick through the news channels on the room's TV, and a couple of pills to settle her digestive later, Thumper bounded down to join Magin in the garden as he was catching the shattering petals of a rose.

'Want to try the car again?' she sang out.

The agent tossed the pink confetti into the air and it rained down over the patient Labrador.

'Yes,' he said. 'Why not.' He strode over to meet her by the Mini.

'Have trouble sleeping?'

'No.' He smiled. 'I never tried to.'

'Went on a nature ramble instead, did you?'

'Something like that.'

She didn't believe him; he looked too immaculate to have explored the brambles and nettles around there. 'Never fell down any deep holes in the dark, then.'

'No. Though it's interesting, mineralogy isn't really my subject.'

Thumper scowled. 'Just where have you been, you beggar?'

Magin's polite manner had an ominous, unworldly edge to it. 'Have you ever noticed how much Nature perfumes the night air?'

'I'm not a nocturnal bee!' Thumper snapped like an enraged Alice confronting the Mad Hatter.

'Oh, don't be annoyed.'

'If you're really a botanist I'm Mary Quant.'

'Look,' Magin pulled something from his inside pocket and handed it to her. 'A peace offering.'

The sight of it momentarily put Thumper off guard. 'That's an ammonite! You never had that when we searched you?'

'I found it.'

'Lying sod.' She tried to hand it back. He wouldn't accept it, so she pushed it into her pocket. 'Let's start moving.'

Having gone through the performance of putting her duffle bag on the back seat, checking the mirrors, and fastening her seatbelt, Thumper turned on the ignition. She expected to hear its familiar spluttering, but there was no such luck. She had never driven a Rolls, but the purring of the machine made her immediately suspect Magin had put the engine of one under the bonnet.

There was nothing else for it but to pull out onto the road.

'I didn't know you were a mechanic?' Thumper snarled.

Magin just shrugged in mock modesty, not displaying so much as a grease stain on his clothes for the effort.

CHAPTER 32

When Mital and Alvas returned, they removed their overgowns and joined Forram. Despite his erratic state of mind, they saw no reason to delay their investigation. Almost half of the crystals had been recorded and his testimony would easily fill the others.

As Alvas was setting up the next crystal, a tall figure suddenly appeared in the entrance to the chamber. She was in the same age group as the Park Keeper, but could not have been more contrasting in looks and manner. Thin, wiry and commanding in an uncompromising sort of way, the only flexible movement the travel technician's limbs seemed to make was when she pulled back the heavy curtain to stop the heat from escaping.

'Sorry, didn't mean to interrupt.' Cloval sounded as though that had been her sole intention.

Forram involuntarily shrank back at her approach.

The travel technician gave a cruel smile. 'Still spinning "what might have beens", I see.'

'Leave him alone,' scolded the Park Keeper. 'He never interfered when you were testifying.'

'It's all right,' said Forram. 'I have nothing to fear. Whatever else may be happening to my brain, it still knows the difference between truth and fantasy.'

'Truth!' Cloval laughed. 'I'm sure it'll take more than your "truth" to put this pathetic civilisation to rights.'

'We have no reason to doubt Monitor Forram's

integrity.' Mital had surprising authority in her voice for one so young.

'Why not just prosecute me and get it over with?' Cloval challenged, fully aware that advanced age put her above a law which was made before it occurred to anyone that characters like her could exist.

'You are exempt because you are a travel technician and above the age of majority,' Alvas explained patiently, wishing he could find just one thing that would enable him to make her take the blame for something: bad manners on this scale should have been against the law.

'There you are, Cloval,' laughed the Park Keeper. 'Pity neither of us have the energy or imagination to get up to anything worth being prosecuted for.'

'Speak for yourself, you silly old fool.'

The Park Keeper's tone hardened. 'I could even break both your spindly legs in front of these representatives of the law, and only have to fill in a form to say that I'm above the age of legal responsibility.'

The Park Keeper certainly had the strength to carry out her threat; it would have probably been with the approval of everyone there as well.

Forram gave a small giggle. 'That wouldn't slow her down. She'd just hobble into the transmission portal and steal a pair of wings from somewhere. The way she's jerked her DNA about in there, it's a wonder she never came back fitted with wheels.'

'Given your state of mind, they'll have you banished and working down the next shaft they sink for city foundations,' snarled Cloval, 'Try talking yourself out of that with a lobotomy.'

The Park Keeper lost patience with her old friend. 'Oh go away Cloval,' she told her. 'Come up later when you're in a better mood and we'll share some broth.'

Having made her point and exhausted her invective, the travel technician strode out as suddenly as she had arrived.

Mital was used to the eccentric behaviour that made

adults so unreliable. 'Are you ready to go on, Monitor Forram?'

'All right,' he agreed reluctantly. They were only half way through the interview and he was already exhausted.

CHAPTER 33

The air was rippling around the vase in the folly and bird song in the immediate area was subdued - even the starlings had stopped squabbling.

Daffy's flesh began to creep as though she had walked into that strange, creepy silence that can follow a horrible accident.

Against every rational instinct telling her not to, she watched indistinguishable shapes writhing faintly in the disturbed air like hyperactive amoeba on a slide. She hoped that they were her imagination, or only the distorted images of technicians reflected through the Hell Well. Anything else was too horrible to contemplate.

Daffy decided not to ask Cloval when she returned. This house guest was tangible, only slightly alien, and bad-tempered enough to be from a comfortably convergent species. The technology she treated in such a cavalier manner was a horse of a different cosmic colour, though.

Daffy shuddered and turned back to the house. Her subconscious horrors were not going to allow her to rationalise this strange pandemonium into something that could be taken in her stride.

A mile away, military surveillance teams still scanned the area. Fortunately Sovariagn transmission beams were far beyond the capability of their technology to detect, otherwise Daffy would have had something more substantial than Cloval on the doorstep.

An army tank would have just fitted comfortably on her front lawn.

CHAPTER 34

In the garden far above the glittering metropolis, five voiceless scouts stopped their respective tasks to stand and listen. The mysterious ability that linked their thoughts told them that one of their number had died. As though compensation for losing the implants that defined their existence, Nature had given them a shared telepathic ability. Keeping it from Forram's technicians was difficult, but preferable to dissection. Only D24 had not yet learnt how to conceal that light of comprehension in its eyes, but it would eventually come.

The scouts left their gardening tools in tidy piles and furtively ascended to the highest point of the garden. None of them knew when one of them had discovered the entrance to the cave. It was some while ago and the defective unit long dead.

Whenever the Park Keeper was occupied with visitors, the scouts frequently made their ways down that secret sloping tunnel into the Iglatte temple. The ancient cave was gently illuminated by the rock's phosphorescence. It had been one of the last strongholds of a subterranean people unable to hold out against the dominant Sovariagn species, the ones who had named the planet after themselves.

The scouts had placed the skeletons of the small massacred creatures littering the floor in simple niches cut high in the walls, as this was apparently the ancient Iglatte custom. Then they cleaned the artefacts of the temple. So it became the scouts spiritual home, though not where they worshipped. It was difficult for creatures like the defective units to believe in any deity, benevolent or otherwise, and the Sovariagn denied that any scout could have had a soul.

This was where they came to share thoughts.

The Iglatte temple filled by the ghosts of a benign people was reassuring. Here, out of everyone else's gaze, the defective scouts didn't have to think about their bizarre appearances, or the abilities they had lost in having their implants removed.

Their strangeness was ironically more obvious when they gathered together in one place, and the only thing they had in common was the need to balance on two legs. However sophisticated the Sovariagn believed their society to be, they did not investigate worlds where the inhabitants were too alien. The scales, spines, oval skulls and double eyelids of these units they could just about cope with in small doses. Tentacles, fangs, more than four genders, nebulosity, and slime they could not.

The Sovariagn were also wary of the supernatural. Belief in it was strictly controlled and anyone accused of telepathy or clairvoyance was monitored to make sure they never spread the contagion.

D20 checked that the tunnel entrance was sealed and secure while the other four positioned themselves in a circle around the rim of the basin that housed the temple's most sacred artefact. The earlier scouts had originally assumed the column of colours spiralling up from its centre to be gas escaping from deep in the planet's crust. Then, instinctively, they had linked hands about it. One of the group on watch outside the circle, to its terror, realised that its thoughts had been linked to beings in another dimension and projected into the basin below.

That was when the defective scouts discovered that they had the power to watch any world in the Galaxy more efficiently than the travel technicians with their transmit routes and bioengineered creatures like them. The tiny, ancient Iglatte had solved the problem the travel technicians had worked aeons on, and the result had been inherited by the very creatures the Sovariagn exploited as biological machines.

Standing apart from the gathering, D20 conjured up the lodge antechamber where D16's body lay. It had been cocooned for burial. That meant Forram's technicians had no interest in dissecting it.

Then mischief took over.

D20 concentrated to the limit of its powers until its thoughts were linked to another world; the one that had caused those young people to visit their garden to investigate why the portal on it was so dramatically closed.

The planet only had one sun and one moon and its continents were sprawled untidily to one side of its globe like rounded-up leviathans. Its elegantly simple calendar put the complex Sovariagn way of keeping time to shame.

D20 pinpointed the decommissioned portal, which was situated in the overgrown grounds of the manor.

The Georgian folly where it had been was now surrounded by a jungle of bracken and autumn's first fierce winds had brought down the pavilion's roof. To ensure that the route would never be reopened, the travel technicians had overturned and broken the large granite vase inside it. Now leaves were cascading from the trees as though intent on burying the scene of a crime.

A short distance away, on the other side of a small orchard, was a house. Dogs ran barking and rolling through the leaves and from inside the shed attached to the house came a faint hum. Sitting amongst barrels of apples, was an ample young woman busily fashioning clay on a rotating table. Watching intently was a thin, fair-haired companion, and two dogs too old for racing and chasing.

'Oh that's wonderful, Thumper,' said Veronica. 'Don't touch it any more. It's just right to key in the relief.'

Thumper groaned. 'How many more have we got to do?'

'Well, we've fired fifty. Three of them cracked and fourteen more are drying.'

'Christ. One hundred and thirty nine to go.'

'Think of how much we're getting for them.'

'It's the only thing that keeps me going.'

'If we get another batch like this we'll be able to go to Wales for that holiday.'

Thumper sighed. 'I may not be able to go after all.'

'Why not?'

'It's Aunt Daffy.'

Veronica was puzzled. 'What's wrong with her? She seems all right to me.'

Thumper shrugged. 'I don't know. She seems to be getting more distant.'

'Not becoming a born again Christian, is she?'

'I shouldn't think so. We're direct descendants from the first nonconformists. It's probably nothing, but something about her bothers me.'

'What?'

Thumper was quiet for a moment. She knew Veronica could be trusted, yet it seemed unfair to confide in her. 'She sometimes seems to be listening to someone. When I come into a room unexpectedly, it's almost as though she's snapping out of a trance.'

'Well, that secret agent you told me about is probably still on her mind.'

Veronica knew nothing about what had really happened.

The young women had started a promising business together, and telling her that she and her aunt had met an alien would probably persuade even the enthusiastic Veronica that they were both mentally unstable. However traumatic at the time, Aunt Daffy was usually more resilient than this. She should have stopped thinking about what happened to Magin by now. It wasn't like her.

'Perhaps she needs a holiday?' Veronica suggested.

'I hope not. I don't think I could cope with the dogs by myself and watch the kiln as well.'

Veronica pinched the finishing touches into the small porcelain figure she had been working on and held it up. 'Look.'

'What on earth is that?'

'I'm not sure, but it's got lots of hair and wings.'

Thumper gingerly took it from her. 'Where do you get your ideas from?'

'I don't know. That one just occurred to me.'

Thumper looked at it long and hard. 'Do you ever have the feeling that something's haunting you?' she asked.

One of the porcupines pushed its snout into a crack and began to munch noisily.

'Ugh!' Veronica leapt up. 'Porky's found a slug!'

'Serve it right.' Thumper handed the small figure back so she could cut her pot from the wheel.

D20 and its companions then watched Daffy exercising four of the larger dogs in the overgrown estate. She was walking the route of the telegraph poles as though expecting a message to be mysteriously transmitted through their non-existent lines.

The autumn gales had died down and a hazy sun appeared. The ground wasn't muddy yet, but summer had picked up her rosy skirts and bolted weeks ago. Daffy had believed that her uneasiness would fade with the season. However, like the menopause, such processes were erratic in passing.

She often pictured her Christopher, perhaps washed ashore on some desolate island, but this time her apprehensions were not for him. The thoughts niggling at the back of Daffy's mind were too strange to make sense of.

D20 tried with all the telepathic might it possessed to make itself known.

Daffy hesitated by a Scots pine and looked blankly down at last year's cones. She sensed a wordless message slip away and knew, however hard she tried to retrieve it, the thought would never return.

D20 toppled over and lay motionless, breaking the other defective units' circle.

Eventually D20 came to, regretting its journey into dimensions that shouldn't have concerned it. Now D16 was gone, the link was not strong enough to make such ambitious contacts.

D24 would never take its place. Apart from its problem with the temperature, the scout would never recover from losing its implants despite Surgeon Arbel trying to do her best for it.

D20 made its shaky way out of the temple and sat in the garden while the others gathered together the twigs and flowers needed for a simple funeral service. The Sovariagn had rationalised the loss of loved ones as being part of evolution. Not having much time for spirits, they tended to keep death in the closet, polished with lack of sentiment. They would have taken a dim view of the defective scouts' tender concern for a departed companion.

CHAPTER 35

The only thing Thumper could do about the obliging tiger roaring away under the bonnet of her Mini was silently curse.

She took as many detours as she dared without pushing her luck too far. Magin probably had a compass inside his head as well as a motor mechanic's manual. Each of them knew the game the other was playing, and Thumper wished she was as good at it as Aunt Daffy. At least she wouldn't have felt so out of her depth.

By midmorning they were driving along a coast road.

Magin watched the sun's rays sparkling on the ripples of the sea and seemed transfixed by the wheeling of the gulls as though they were a new experience. Thumper assumed he didn't get out much. She was too focused on what she was doing to wonder about the contradictions in his character any longer.

'How much further?' Magin inquired with a curious lack of insistence.

'Almost there. Though I can't be sure about the exact spot until we arrive.'

'Ah, we're going to have a game of hunt the alien.'

Thumper slammed on the brakes so hard only the seat belts stopped them from hitting the windscreen. 'Do you or do you not want to carry on?'

He knew she was only bluffing for time, but Magin

couldn't resist shrugging his shoulders. 'Why spoil the game after coming this far?'

'That does it!'

She pulled over to a lay-by where a fly-tipper had thoughtfully left a large armchair, door-less deep freezer, and much-soiled mattress for the benefit of the wildlife. Judging by the empty plastic containers littering the grass verge, the deep freeze had contained something a local fox found worth prizing them open for, and rats were using the mattress as a dormitory. Nothing so far had found use for the armchair. Its faded, red velvet upholstery remained intact.

'Nice view,' observed Magin looking over the rubbish towards the sea.

That was too much for Thumper. She grabbed her duffle bag, jumped out of the Mini, slammed the door, and marched to the top of the hill on the other side of the road. She knew Magin would eventually have to follow her. The further away she was by then, the more time it would buy.

Thumper was soon out of breath. She glanced back down at the coast road. Magin was lounging in the armchair, watching an untidy circle of screaming swifts high above. The postmistress once had a cat that would study any out of reach bird with the same hypnotic gaze. That used to let out the occasional bleat of chagrin because it couldn't reach them, though. When Magin observed things, he was a tombstone. Thumper wouldn't have been surprised if he'd picked up the habit through hiding behind so many, because there was something of the graveyard about his demeanour. He would have made a splendid undertaker; black crepe was invented for him.

Thumper shuddered, and then bounded over the summit of the hill and out of his sight. She sat down on a handy clump of grass and pulled out of her duffle bag the sandwiches Daffy had made for her in the event of just such an emergency.

CHAPTER 36

D24 began to cough with painfully hollow convulsions.

The sound broke Forram's train of thought. He stopped giving his statement and went to the defective unit.

Alvas switched off the recording crystal.

'What is wrong with it?' asked Mital.

'Scar tissue in D24's lungs. Have to be removed when it's strong enough.'

'Keeps coughing until I ventilate it,' added the Park Keeper. 'The unit will lie so awkwardly.'

Mital was unable to understand why the scout was there at all, given its condition. 'Shouldn't it really be in more comfortable quarters? This can hardly be the ideal environment.'

For some things, youth was no excuse and Forram became annoyed. 'Have you ever been inside a cubicle used to treat defective scouts?'

Mital sensed that she was on dangerous ground. 'Would it be better if we went outside for a short while?'

The Park Keeper was pulling a ventilator from its case and neither of the young people was keen on seeing it used, even on a defective scout.

The Park Keeper was grateful that the young interrogators wanted to leave. Both of them and their recording crystals were getting on her nerves. 'Good idea. It won't take long. While you're out there you might look around for the robot. Its signal went dead shortly after it nearly collided with you.'

This filled Alvas and Mital with even more apprehension. As the ventilator's mask was clamped to D24's face, they darted outside with as much dignity as they could.

The suddenness of the crisp air was refreshing after the lodge's stifling heat. They hastily fastened their overgowns and followed a narrow track up into the densely vegetated area of the garden. Being so steep, it was the most unlikely place for the faulty robot to have blundered and they certainly didn't want to run into it again.

The twisting branches wove eerie shadows and the path's frosted chippings crunched and sparkled like salt crystals. Long tubular flowers gave off an acrid aroma that, for all their beauty, was overpowering enough to deter the most enthusiastic pollinator. It was probably the creation of some medical chemist who had found a use for its pungent perfume.

'Where are we?' Alvas tried not to sound as though it mattered too much.

'The Lower Lights.' Mital was too absorbed with their mysterious surroundings to elaborate.

'Lower Lights? This must be one of the highest points in the park?'

'It is. This is where the chemists grow all the plants most people prefer not to see. There is a network of screens to deflect intense sunlight and lower the light levels. Most of the plants are very valuable.' Mital pointed to some black domes sitting like fungi in the dell below them. 'The ones in there are grown for research. However fit we become, their genes will never be allowed to die.'

The young people went down to touch the domes. They had an unpleasantly organic feel. The growths nursed so lovingly inside them had evolved in the planet's deepest caves and would have shrivelled under Sovariagn's suns.

'Are these the plants the Iglatte used to farm?'

'It was their staple diet apparently,' said Mital.

'No wonder they lost the will to live.'

'Their extermination had more to do with their reluctance to allow us to mine the mineral veins they lived in.'

Alvas was horrified. 'No, really?'

'According to the classified history teacher. Apparently our ancestors poisoned the rivers which ran through their tunnel networks. Those that didn't die were compelled to come above ground and be dehydrated by the sunlight.'

Alvas began to wonder if Mital had been contaminated

by the freethinking Park Keeper and Cloval. 'I don't believe it.'

Although only fractionally older, Mital often found his grasp of the real world naive. 'You're sounding like an adult. How do you think our species became wealthy enough to afford such delicate morals? We used to be pirates.'

Alvas was appalled, more by her attitude than the forbidden facts she was blithely spilling out as though in response to a minor verbal exam. Mital had always been acknowledged as the more sensitive; now she was sounding like an above-ager who had been there, seen that, and done it all. For her, the age of majority was closer than she realised.

'Don't talk like that,' Alvas told her severely and passed on to a cream-coloured dome. 'What's in here?'

Mital knew that it been an error of judgement to burden Alvas's immature sensibilities with such horrible truths, and she dropped the subject. 'Only protein plants. The Park Keeper grows them for the defective scouts. Some of them have trouble digesting after their implants have been removed.'

'And the next one?'

'That's out of bounds. The pollinators in there have a fatal sting.'

'No wonder they're tucked out of the way.' Alvas was now totally unsettled. He preferred to wait as long as possible before becoming an adult. 'Let's go back up. I don't like this place.' He lifted the hem of his long overgown and strode back up the path. Then something caught his attention. 'What are those?' He indicated the cup-like indentations between the trunks of some trees.

'Graves. The Park Keepers bury the defective scouts here because they aren't allowed to incinerate them. Whenever these trees come into flower, they shed their petals into those shallow wells. They remain fresh until the next time they flower.'

Alvas examined a grave and a small pool of glittering

orange petals more closely. 'It's very quiet up here - too quiet.'

'We're well above most noise.'

'I find this type of burial distasteful. They should be cocooned and allowed to fall to dust.'

'They have no families to add them to their pantheon. At least these graves mark their existence.' Mital felt a disconcerting surge of empathy for the alien creatures. 'It's strange, when the old Park Keeper told me all this, I didn't understand what she meant. It seems quite sad now.'

Alvas was unable to comprehend her concern. After all, they were only biologically engineered units - so many rearranged genes, like those living ships the Hysocs use. When one dies, they just grow another.

Alvas looked up as he realised that they were being watched.

The young couple turned and saw the inquisitive, angelic expression of D20 looking a little too self-aware for comfort. Behind it were four other scouts.

'We've interrupted something,' Mital whispered. Alvas would have hastily left. 'No, it's all right. They're quite harmless.' Mital discretely went over to where the defective scouts were clustered about an empty grave. The alien expressions looked on benignly as she stooped to examine the inscription on its rim. 'Sentinel Sathe Dex Luin.'

'Sathe Dex Luin?' echoed Alvas.

'D16.'

'Oh yes, it used to have a name, didn't it.'

Mital reassuringly touched D20's fine hair. 'We should leave now.'

Alvas wanted to repeat that they were only biological machines after all, but was not able to and silently went down the track after Mital.

They would have gone straight back to the Park Keeper's lodge if they hadn't come across some tracks that veered to the cliff's edge. They were scoured deep into the ground.

'I think we might have discovered the Park Keeper's robot.'

The thought that the hateful machine had met some mishap filled Alvas with the sort of vindictive satisfaction not encouraged in young people of his calling.

The tracks had become deeper as the machine's brakes failed and, at the edge of the cliff, a large wedge of rock had been bitten out.

They peered down. A long way below, they could just make out the smashed remains of the robot, the missing piece of cliff clenched firmly in all its claws.

Mital sighed. 'Oh dear. The Park Keeper isn't going to like this.'

'How far down do you think it is?'

'Too far for her hoist to reach it.' Mital pulled a small transmitter from her belt and keyed in some instructions.

'Who are you calling?'

'Cleansing. They're all robots, so they might as well pick up the remains of this one.'

'She may want to give it a decent burial.'

'Once she sees the new unit we ordered, I guarantee she'll soon forget this one.'

Alvas looked down dubiously at the tangle of cogs, armour and wheels, and then noticed the magical scene far beyond it. 'Isn't it wonderful how the metropolis gleams from up here.'

'You'll soon be able to go back down, though I quite like it up here myself.'

'This place is eerie, full of the dead and haunted.'

'That's why it doesn't get many visitors.'

Alvas noticed someone moving on one of the paths below. 'There's one.'

Mital saw a figure wearing a loose thermal gown. 'So there is. Looks like one of the senior chemists.'

'Might be here to check on the medicine weeds.'

'Don't let a chemist hear you call them that. They have a paranoid respect for plants.'

The chemist was only taking a leisurely stroll in his casual, patterned gown and loose slippers, having just disembarked from the mountain lift. Not many people tackled the thousands of steps up unless they had someone to impress or something to prove.

'They must have finished working on D24 by now. Let's get back,' insisted Alvas.

CHAPTER 37

Keeping one eye on the summit of the hill above her the other on the pickle dripping from her sandwich, Thumper received the fright of her life when a soft voice just below her said, 'I'm sure there must be more comfortable places to stop for lunch.'

She nearly choked. 'How did you get up here without me seeing you, you swine?'

'I dematerialised.'

It was easy to believe that there was something supernatural about Magin. 'Now try flying off a cliff.'

For a moment Thumper wondered why she disliked the man so much. He was only doing his job after all. Twenty years younger and she might have actually fancied him with a bottle of Daffy's raspberry wine inside her.

Then the drip of cold pickle on Thumper's wrist reminded her that they were trying to keep Cloval out of this elegant spider's mandibles.

'I'm still not going on.' Thumper took another bite of the sandwich.

Magin sat a discrete distance away. 'I may not be your idea of the perfect human being, but there are far worse, I assure you. Your alien would be much safer with me than those others. Once I know where he is, I can give him protection.'

'The only person he needs protecting from is you. I would never have agreed to do this if it weren't for Aunt Daffy.'

'She understands the power of the military. None of us are safe from them.'

'And how can I be sure you even belong to this country? There is something bloody weird about you.'

'So that makes me a foreigner? I wouldn't have thought you were the sort to hold other nationalities in contempt?'

He was right, there was nothing xenophobic about Thumper, yet that wasn't the point. 'And why should I trust you? You're too smooth to need talcum powder. It's wrong, what I'm doing. I want him to get away from this planet altogether.'

'Would nothing I say would be the truth to you? Sometimes things aren't quite what they seem.'

'Oh come on - don't tell me you're here to help? You're enough to make my old teddy bear suspicious. I've seen reptiles with less sinister profiles.'

'And all reptiles have to be trodden on.'

'I never said that. Stop putting words into my mouth.'

'With the amount of food in it, they wouldn't stand a chance.'

'Oh ha, bloody ha!' Thumper pulled herself together before she threw something at him. As there were only a few buttercups and a pickle sandwich to hand, she would have looked pretty silly. 'What else do I need to trust you about, anyway? We're telling you all we know.'

Magin stretched his long legs and lay against the steep slope of the hill. 'Every lizard needs a bolthole.'

Thumper as last understood what he was inferring. 'You mean... someone's after you?'

'My wretched occupation, you see.'

'And if they are, what can I do about it? '

'I wouldn't be so unreasonable as to expect you to hide me from my pursuers. That would be beyond dangerous. Perhaps forgetting that you ever set eyes on me, or at least what direction I left in when this is all over, might help.'

Thumper hesitated. 'You're having me on?'

Magin got up, brushed the grass seeds from his

trousers and fastened his coat. 'I will take that as a "no, you do not trust me".'

Thumper felt embarrassed; she didn't know why. 'Well, what am I supposed to say?'

'Finish your sandwich before I start trying to put words into your mouth again.'

'Oh... Piss off! '

With a sarcastic half bow, Magin left.

Thumper had lost her appetite. She fed the remains of the sandwich to the gulls, and then wandered off after him.

When she reached the bottom of the hill he was once again lounging in the armchair like the melancholy ruler of some fiefdom recently defeated in battle. It could have all been an act, though Thumper now had the sneaking suspicion that something was genuinely bothering him. Her attempts to upset him were like mercury rolling from polished marble, but someone more accomplished than her had apparently managed it.

'So what's liable to happen to you if you don't find this alien?'

'There is no reason for you to be concerned. You would believe nothing I told you anyway, and it's probably safer if you don't.'

It must have been a ruse to gain her sympathy. 'Please yourself.' Thumper climbed into the driver's seat. 'Get in then.'

They drove on in silence. Magin's expression was distant as he watched the occasional terrace of cottages and trees that hid the sea pass by.

Their elbows virtually touching, Thumper felt an inexplicable dread. What had she and Aunt Daffy taken on? If there were agents more daunting than Magin waiting in the wings, the sooner they got the business over with and quit the stage the better.

To Magin's surprise, she put her foot down for the few remaining miles. He gave a wry smile. Her anxiety to reach their destination wasn't for his benefit.

Once again the sea came into view.

Thumper turned off the main road and drove to the edge of a pebble shore scattered with boulders.

'We'll have to walk from here.'

'All right,' agreed Magin.

'Nearest railway station is 15 miles across country; no other transport - and you know how unlikely it is that a public telephone would work, even if you could find one.' She nearly added, 'Now don't you wish you'd brought the mobile? '

Thumper got out of the car and led Magin towards a network of caves set just above the high water mark. Common sense should have told her that she was over egging a half-baked cake and that Magin wasn't taken in for a second.

The agent smiled to himself, doubting that any alien would have been desperate enough to clamber into one of those treacherous caverns to hide.

Magin looked down at Thumper as though for the first time. Overall, she didn't seem that bothered by him, only sporadically annoyed. The way she smiled insolently back suggested she was more worried about stepping on a crab.

'He was left somewhere in one of these caves. You can search them if you like.'

'Now what would have brought him to a bleak place like this?' mused Magin. 'It couldn't have been to catch a ferry.'

Thumper was about to oblige him with a tale of how components had collected for the alien so he could set up some sort of fantastic equipment. Then realised just in time that Magin was leading her on and that she might have to prove it.

'So how would I know?' she shrugged.

'You seem confident they'll be no alien?'

'Would I have brought you out here if I thought she-' It was inevitable his relaxed manner would encourage a slip of the tongue sooner or later. '-he was still about.'

Thumper took a deep breath. 'Work the rest out for

yourself.'

Magin strode off, easily negotiating the rocks and channels, looking into every nook and cranny with those gleaming amber eyes. Thumper sat on the bonnet of the car and watched from a distance, amazed at the way he passed over the craterous ground with the agility of a panther. His frock coat flared out behind him as he jumped sure-footedly from rock to rock.

Then Magin appeared to find something. Although she couldn't be sure what it was at first, Thumper felt her heart bounce. The object was silver and shone just like the pouch Cloval had given to Aunt Daffy. Their only hope now was that he would recognise it as alien.

Magin made his way back to the car, thoughtfully examining his find.

'I'm glad you weren't lying to me Thumper.'

'You sure about that then?'

'The material was not manufactured on this planet.'

'You can tell that, can you? Carry a book of fabric samples around in your head as well?'

'You can easily assess the properties of stone and pottery. I have a few such abilities myself.'

'I believe you.' Thumper slid off the bonnet and sat in the front seat of the Mini. 'I'll wait here if you're going to poke around some more.'

Magin carefully folded the pouch and placed it inside his coat then returned to his search.

Thumper sighed with heartfelt relief when he was out of earshot. 'Thank you Eccles!'

She waited until he was far away, searching the pebbles of the rocky beach.

Then she started the car's engine and drove off as fast as its new least of life would allow.

CHAPTER 38

At last free of her surgical duties, Arbel stood in the crystal garden on the roof of her home gazing at the skyline.

The metropolis was shaped like a dome, the glittering citadel crowning its summit. She wondered why it was necessary for everything on Sovariagn to glitter so much. From its glaciers to silicon deserts, mountains to glass-like seas, everything about Sovariagn gleamed as though its perpetual sunlight had burnished it. Other civilisations swore that cosmic tinsel haloed the people as well. Not that many visited the intimidating world and its aloof occupants. They preferred their extraterrestrial contacts to be hands on, and not through genetically manipulated spies. As a consequence, the mythology about the Sovariagn had grown. Some of it touched on the inevitable truth that had just crashed down on Arbel. Now the surgeon was all too aware of the cracks in this world of dazzling ice that claimed unsuspecting conformists like her devoted Forram. What would his technicians do without him when he did eventually lose his mind? Arbel had never encountered anyone who was mad. Perhaps there was another secret mountain garden like the one for defective scouts to keep society's other embarrassments out of sight - and another for those with speech impediments, baldness, limps or bicoloured eyes. Cupboards in the cloudless sky for the less than perfect.

Arbel shuddered. Once she would have laughed at such a thought. Since then her idyllic perceptions had been dealt a blow. She might have been able to rationalise them: few other Sovariagn were capable of questioning the status quo. If it was the law, then it was right.

Arbel ran her fingers over the bloom of the tree Forram had planted in honour of her medical accomplishments. She plucked a stamen with surgical precision and wondered how well the diminishing wits of her husband were holding up under the interrogation of the metropolis' best investigators. No scream for help had been received during her absence, from either Forram or the two young people with him. Perhaps she needn't have feared so much for her husband's sanity after all.

As Arbel went below she could hear her son rummaging about in his quarters, busily preparing to leave before his father returned. She went to the letter recorder and thoughtfully dictated a message. After it was printed out in her immaculate script, she sealed it.

'Delas,' Arbel called.

The activity in her son's quarters stopped. The screen separating his rooms from the rest of the group parents' apartments was raised.

'Will you go on an errand for me?'

'Of course mother.'

Arbel held out an oval key. 'This will operate the lift.'

The youth's expression clouded.

'I want you to give this letter to your father.' She handed the message to him. 'I have a pressing matter to attend to and the note is urgent.'

'Can't you send it through the recorder, or order a robot to take it?' he pleaded desperately.

'No. You must hand it to him yourself. You cannot hate him forever, Delas, you don't have that sort of stamina.'

'I'll never forgive him.'

'If you were his age and in his position you would have done exactly the same. Your virtuous anger will not help D24 now.'

'He could have let it die. That's what it wanted.'

'Would you take its life?'

Delas was silent for a while. 'How could I? It was my friend.'

'Soon you will see it as just another scout, a defective unit to be put out of sight and forgotten.'

'Never.'

'Believe me, when you reach your majority you will eventually regard it as most others do - an alien machine.'

'I don't think it knows me any more.'

'It knows you. The only compensation those wretched creatures are allowed to keep is their memories. Now please go Delas.'

The youth felt guilty because he knew she was right.

Delas pulled on an overgown and silently left.

Arbel switched on her diary and listened to a strangely attractive voice. The way the scout had used the Sovariagn tongue was seductive. It was a tragedy that its alien phenotype was so unattractive. Would her conscience have been moved sooner if the creature were beautiful, with golden body hair and wings like D20? Perhaps the technicians had subconsciously looked for that small mental imbalance in D24? Who were the Sovariagn to judge what other species should behave and look like, though? D24's act of rebellion was probably part of its phenotype and out of its control.

Arbel reached for her overgown.

She went down to the gleaming pavements and footbridges of the metropolis. The domes, spires and towers that had once been so familiar, were now a dimension away. She passed by people who had known her most of her life as though in a trance. Life seemed to be slowing down.

By the time she reached the citadel, nothing sparkled any more. All Arbel could see was the hypocritical, emotional dross that had encrusted Sovariagn for centuries.

CHAPTER 39

Magin turned in bland surprise to watch Thumper drive off. He laughed at himself for not being more prepared. Perhaps he had managed to persuade himself that Thumper trusted him just a fraction. But it didn't matter. Nothing much mattered any longer.

The agent rolled down his sleeves and looked about. Those circling swifts still screamed out their mockery.

And, on a promontory overlooking the beach, was Colonel Angela Tovey.

As she peered through binoculars she must have realised that he was laughing at her. He sensed how annoyed she was and, about to wave, thought better of it. If there was one thing Colonel Tovey loathed above all others, it was the quarry refusing to take her pursuit of them seriously; it made her trigger finger twitch. The man wouldn't be treating her with this level of contempt if she had been a freelance.

It would have been easier to follow Magin's plump girlfriend in the souped-up Mini, but he wouldn't have let her go so easily if she had known anything of value.

While relieved that the military agent hadn't gone after Thumper, this left Magin with a problem. He couldn't afford to let Colonel Tovey see what he was about to do.

Magin nonchalantly strolled off. He walked up the coast road and carried on along the cliff, his black frock coat fluttering against the backdrop of the sky filled with swifts and gulls like the slash of a furious voter on a blue ballot paper.

He would be visible for miles now, so Colonel Tovey took the opportunity to make for her car. If Magin had a backup vehicle, she would have seen it from her vantage point. The agent drove her car from the cover of the gully to the top of the cliffs where she stepped out to see how far Magin had got.

He had only been out of her sight for minutes, but was nowhere to be seen. For miles in either direction there was nothing moving apart from the gulls and swifts scything the cobalt sky.

CHAPTER 40

Although Thumper knew that Magin's adjustments to the Mini would take her all the way home, she wanted to travel in a vehicle that wouldn't be recognised, so drove on to Eccles' studio.

The sculptor's home was perched on a cliff some nineteen miles away. Eccles, now a virtual recluse, was prepared to take this game of Thumper and Daffy's all in good part and was also happy to trust Thumper with her station wagon for a couple of days. Having carted all the stone and plaster, and delivered any completed commissions, Eccles only needed her bike to collect the groceries. Peddling was good therapy for the rheumatism.

The station wagon had suffered quite a battering over the years. It had also been converted into a machine capable of overtaking most other traffic and carrying loads that would have buckled the axle of any normal car.

Higham Grange, perched high on a cliff, had been passed down, rather clumsily, through generations of Eccles' family. She was now the only member of it with enough stamina and stubbornness to live there. The damp sea breezes should have aggravated her rheumatism, yet she hardly felt the twinges when absorbed in her work. This was in such great demand she considered giving up part time teaching and civilisation altogether. Eccles came from the school which believed that true inspiration needed self-denial. Not many modern students were willing to share the same philosophy for the sake of their art and, as a consequence, all ended up teaching. Thumper was one of the few not intimidated by her old tutor or the standards she set, unlike Veronica who had burst into tears when confronted by the pieta Eccles had made for a convent. They both suspected that this modeller of fairy homes and friendly dragons had been frightened by Pre-Raphaelite pictures when young and subdued by Catholic guilt.

Eccles' home may have attracted nesting gulls and

many forms of damp loving life forms, but it was the last place a secret agent would think of investigating - Thumper hoped.

Avoiding discarded lumps of stone and casing materials littering the outer yard, Thumper drove under the arch leading to the house and out of sight of the road.

In her large studio at the back of the courtyard, Eccles was pondering the merits of an oblong shape supporting the sculpture of a jumping antelope.

As Thumper came in Eccles asked without looking up, 'Now what would you do about that?'

'Bush?' suggested Thumper.

'Piece of dead wood? - Keys are on the rhino's nose.'

'Essential?'

Thumper quickly discovered the mighty marble creature waiting to charge an inoffensive plaster clown and rescued the station wagon keys.

'Holds up statue.'

'What was it meant to be originally?'

'Lion.'

'Lion?'

'Stone split. Flawed all the way through. It's that lump of detritus laying outside.'

'Really Eccles, you shouldn't be lugging stone that heavy about.'

'Stop nagging, you little pot-thrower and think of something useful.'

Thumper had a flash of inspiration. 'Striking snake - Thanks for doing the envelope by the way.'

Snakes of many shapes and sizes had already occurred to Eccles, but if Thumper couldn't think of anything better, snake it would have to be. 'Have to be a fat one then - It's okay, I needed the exercise, anyway.'

'You cycled all the way out there!'

'And back. Better than any physio. Hope you win your game, or whatever it is.'

'Looks as though we will now. Our fox doesn't have a bike.'

'What's it all about anyway?'

'Hunt the alien.'

'Foreign or metaphysical?'

'Extraterrestrial.'

'Do me some sketches.'

'She's a bit scraggy. Lots of hair.'

'Well, I've always wanted to do a Bernini before my wrists go. Got several blocks of marble to use up.'

'And she's bad-tempered. We have to keep her in the deep freeze.'

'She won't fancy having a cast taken then?'

'Doubt it. If the fellow chasing me turns up, you could always ask him. Got a profile like a pterodactyl. Pity he wasn't around when you were doing the relief for the fossil room of that natural history museum.' Thumper stamped to remove some dry plaster from her feet and stone dust cascaded from the rafters.

'Careful. Not too sure what I've got stored up there.'

'I'll bring the station wagon back some time tomorrow or the day after.'

'Fine, fine.' Eccles was still concentrating on the antelope. 'Take your time. Tank is full.' The sculptor proceeded to rough out a rather plump snake striking at the antelope's hooves.

'See you.' Thumper picked her way back out through the discarded plaster mouldings and stone blocks.

The station wagon was waiting in the drive. Without being laden by brass castings or blocks of stone, even her Mini with Magin's improvements wouldn't have been able to match the sweetness with which it pulled away and sped along the motorway she had so assiduously avoided on the way there.

Magin may have been clever, yet it was difficult to see how he could get out of this one.

Thumper switched on one of Eccles' tapes and drove home to the strains of Telemann and Vivaldi in a fraction of the time it had taken her on the way out. She was back home by mid-afternoon.

Daffy couldn't quite believe that things had gone so smoothly. Magin must have suspected what they were up to, yet she was still not prepared to allow Cloval to visit the pavilion portal.

As soon as Thumper had settled down with a stout ale, Daffy went out to look for the tell tale signs which would indicate that the transmit beam was operational. If she saw anything alien, whether travel technician or recall collar, she was to dash straight back and fetch her.

Careful not to break the security beam Cloval had circled the pavilion with, Daffy ascertained that the lid of the vase was now suspended on a cushion of air a couple of centimetres above its rim. The link had been re-established, but there was no sign of any technician or recall unit.

A sudden rustling in the bracken behind the pavilion made Daffy quickly turn. She went to investigate.

It was only Porky and Pine.

'What the hell are you two doing out here?' she yelled at the porcupines. 'Don't you know that's incest?'

By the vacuous rodent expressions gazing back, it was obvious they weren't too bothered.

'Oh hell,' Daffy cursed to herself. 'Apart from that, it looks bloody painful.' She strode back to the house before she was distracted by anything else in the undergrowth.

'This is... not sensible...' The grasp of Cloval's language implant on the alien language was beginning to slacken. 'The route is obviously open. Something must be preventing them from sending a recall unit through.'

'They've still got plenty of time,' Daffy tried to reassure her. 'Even if Magin has guessed you're here, I'm convinced he was working alone. Thumper's sure no one was following her. You'd best keep cool in the meantime.'

Cloval was persuaded to return to the deep freezer.

Porky and Pine entered through their flap and, feeling peckish after their incest, trotted into the living room.

'Don't let those two in there!' Daffy warned Thumper. 'I left a bowl of cherries on the coffee table.'

Thumper bounded after the porcupines and managed to snatch up the fruit in the nick of time. As she was placing it out of reach on the bookcase someone knocked the front door.

'All straight in there?' she called to Daffy.

'She's locked in. You can answer it.'

Picking up her carton of yoghurt on the way, Thumper went to the front door expecting to see a Jehovah's Witness or window cleaner.

She should have known; a man that clever could never have been tricked so easily.

'Magin! How the Hell?'

CHAPTER 41

Alvas put another crystal in his recorder. 'Is there much more? The allocation is almost full.'

Forram gave the youthful dispenser of justice a faraway look. 'Nothing, but murder.'

'Murder?' Alvas thought for a moment. 'I have heard of this before. Some ancient records refer to this peculiar practice amongst our ancestors. Apparently one of the reasons for our present legal system.'

'What is this "murder" you speak of?' asked Mital.

Technician Cloval hadn't mentioned this archaic act in her statement, but then, she and Forram saw the light of events through prisms distorted to suit them.

It hadn't been Forram's intention to shock them. 'Cloval's human rescuers were bound to be accused of murder after the agent pursuing her was killed.'

Mital relaxed. 'Oh that. The incident has already been well documented.'

'By Cloval, no doubt.'

'We understand how these unfortunate events disturb you, but it is not in our remit. Is there anything you would like to add?'

'No, everything else is on the technicians' recordings.'

Alvas packed his crystals away. 'Thank you Monitor Forram. We hope this matter will be resolved shortly. It appears that you acted properly throughout.'

Mital noticed the desolation in Forram's eyes. 'There is nothing to worry about. We are persuaded that your conduct was correct and you will be totally exonerated.'

Forram shook his head. 'You don't understand, do you?'

Alvas was puzzled by his reaction. Most people were thankful to be exonerated.

'I would rather be as guilty as Cloval.'

This was another conundrum that afflicted those in the age of majority. 'But that would mean banishment for someone your age. Surely there is nothing more important than non-culpability?'

'I am guilty.' Forram wanted to call him a stupid child, but as he had just let him off the hook it would have seemed ungrateful. 'I am guilty of following rules which are without an atom of compassion.'

Mital realised what he was talking about. 'Oh, I see. But that aspect has nothing to do with our brief. Surgeon Arbel is a free agent. I've no doubt she thought that acquiescing to your request to operate on D24 would save the unit from being dealt with by your technicians. I understand that their procedure to remove implants is "businesslike".'

'I should never have asked such a thing of her.'

'No crime has been committed. Defective scout units do not fall within the regulations regarding Sovariagn citizens. They come under "The Protection of Non-Communicating Species". Because of this, what happened to D24 does not warrant an investigation.'

The Park Keeper was becoming exasperated by the young people's conflicting qualities of wisdom and inexperience and, anxious to get rid of them, she helped Mital and Alvas on with their overgowns. 'I'll look after Monitor Forram until Arbel sends someone to fetch him. He'll be all right once everything has settled down.'

'He probably needs a rest,' advised Alvas professionally.

'Yes,' muttered Forram. 'At the bottom of some deep, water-logged mine.'

'What was that?'

'His mind's wandering,' humoured the Park Keeper. 'It's probably out there with all the Iglatte and dead scouts,' she added under her breath.

'Of course. Thank you for your assistance. Not all adults are so co-operative,' he lied.

The young couple left in their infuriatingly dignified way.

Forram did not notice them go. He was watching strange lights inside his eyelids and wondering whether fainting would make them go away.

'Pull yourself together.' The Park Keeper thrust a goblet into his hand. 'The little brat was right. You'll feel better after a rest.'

'I'll never rest until someone removes the implant for conscience.'

'Stop feeling sorry for yourself.'

'I believed in fabulous creatures once, ones which could swaddle the planet with good intentions and save us from our own folly. Perhaps I still believe there should be benign superbeings to save us from having to make the difficult decisions.'

'Where would be the point in incinerating yourself for a defective unit not considered sentient enough to figure in our laws? You heard the child; they come under "The Protection of Non-Communicating Species" - along with anything else that lives in a burrow.'

The Park Keeper poured them both a drink. 'Forget it Forram. Your son will eventually. The young have short memories; as soon as they hit their majority their view of the Universe changes. D24 will only appear more and more grotesque to your child until he wonders why he became a friend of the creature in the first place.'

Forram sipped his drink. 'I did admire D24 in an odd way,' he confessed. 'This scout was unusually astute and possessed strengths neither of us could imagine.

Whatever happened to it on that planet, it was something we could not comprehend.'

'Or perhaps it just became aware of an existence it could never have?'

Forram looked up sharply. 'That would be too horrible to think about. It must have been caught in transmission fluctuations. There can be no other reason why it became so unstable and was unable to contact us.'

'It's dead to all of us now.' The Park Keeper took his goblet and tossed it into the sterilizer. 'I'm the only one who will need to worry about it from now on.'

CHAPTER 42

The eyes of many apprehensive dogs shone from every nook and cranny as Magin strode across the hall towards the kitchen.

'Aunt Daffy! Magin!' Thumper called out, only confirming the agent's suspicions. He was at the kitchen door before it could occur to Thumper to trip him up.

Daffy was nonchalantly wiping her hands on a tea towel. 'Well, well, well.'

'Forgive my sudden intrusion.'

'I was only preparing a bath for one of the dogs. Now you've turned up, I'll never catch it.'

'I'm sure whatever it had wasn't contagious.'

Thumper elbowed her way past him to join Daffy. Her glance spat defiance while her aunt viewed Magin with an infuriating lack of curiosity.

'Rumour has it that the manor house was broken into a couple or so nights ago,' Daffy mentioned as though in passing. 'Very odd. Nothing taken. A lot of dust moved about and armchair uncovered. They did find something interesting though.' The consummate poker player, Magin knew better than to demand what had slipped his needle attention. 'Hair. Several strands of hair had been caught in the studs on a wing of the armchair. Now isn't that interesting.'

'Seems an obsessive sort of inquiry for a non theft.'

'It wasn't that which bothered them. It was wanting to know who could waltz in and out of a zone that secure for the sake of curiosity. With those hairs, the police might just find out. I reckon that could be very embarrassing for someone's department.'

Magin remained expressionless for a moment, and then gave his most charismatic smile. 'Are you blackmailing me, madam?'

Daffy said nothing, just carefully folded the tea towel.

'Yes,' Thumper leapt in, 'You are, aren't you. Or shall I phone the police?'

Knowing Magin wouldn't allow her to pass, Daffy held her niece's arm. 'The army might be more interested.'

Magin seemed to pale a little, yet betrayed nothing.

'What brought you back here, Mr Magin?'

'Fascination. You are both very fascinating creatures.'

'So are you - like a scorpion.'

'I didn't mean to disrupt your blameless idyll. After all, it was only a game, wasn't it? Where is the alien?'

'How should I know?'

'Aunt Daffy, it is not in my brief to harm anyone, but...'

'Don't you threaten me, you satanic reptile - and don't call me Aunt!'

'Where is the alien?'

Thumper sneered. 'You're mad. Where could we be keeping an alien? Search the place if you like.'

'I don't need to, because I would rather you told me. That way no one is liable to get hurt.'

Daffy gave a wry smile that puzzled Magin. 'I thought you would be reduced to revealing your true side sooner or later. Even the most highly polished gemstone has its flaws. '

'There is no more time.'

'Time?'

'You understand what I mean.'

'The portal! He must know it's ready,' whispered

Thumper in alarm.

'Yes, it's ready,' announced Magin. 'Now you have to trust me. Release the alien into my charge.'

'To do what?'

'Trust me.'

Thumper gasped. 'Are you trying to convince us that you'd let it escape?'

'Now I've won the chase, I've no appetite for the kill.'

'Liar! Don't trust him!'

'Just let me speak one word to the creature.'

Despite every instinct telling her not to, Daffy was beginning to have misgivings. 'Why?'

'It might help save a life.'

Daffy quickly came to her senses. 'Oh no, the only life that would save would be yours. If you're so sure of where the alien is, you don't need us to trust you.'

'Well Mr Magin, where is the alien then?' mocked Thumper.

Magin gave up trying to reason with them. 'A creature that came from a cold planet of perpetual daylight would not like being in total darkness for very long.'

'So what?' Thumper couldn't conceal the panic in her voice.

'So why else would you keep the light inside the deep freeze on?'

Daffy and Thumper were caught off guard and Magin took the opportunity to reach out and switch the light on and off. The door opened after the third time.

Thumper desperately hurled herself at the agent and threw him off balance, giving Daffy time to seize the puzzled Cloval and push her out of the back door.

Hardly knowing why, the travel technician ran for her life.

Magin recovered his balance. Thumper blocked his way to prevent him sprinting after Cloval. With a sweep of his fist he struck her on the temple and sent her reeling across the kitchen.

While Thumper lay motionless, Daffy had to let him

dash after Cloval. She didn't believe blood was thicker than water, just that alien blood wasn't thick enough to risk her niece's life for. Fortunately Thumper was only stunned, so Daffy took the spring gun she had primed from its shelf and ran after Magin.

Daffy was far from athletic, but knew every shortcut on the manor house estate and arrived at the activated portal seconds after the other two.

Magin and Cloval were engaged in an odd sort of tussle. It looked as though he was trying to push her into the Hell Well.

She pushed back and suddenly Magin lost his balance, toppling down the pavilion steps. With a brief glance at Daffy, Cloval leapt through the portal and melted from her sight.

Daffy was so amazed at what had happened, she lowered the spring gun. As Magin pulled himself up and came towards her, she raised it again and released the safety catch.

Magin caught his breath. It was the first time she had seen him disorientated.

He quickly recovered his sinister charm. 'What, does the loser have to pay some forfeit?'

'If I were nearer your size ...'

'I know, I deserve a good thrashing, but... I am what I am.'

'You could have killed Thumper, you maniac.'

'Shoot me then,' Magin invited her insolently.

'Why should I? You've lost your alien, haven't you. I've no doubt there are more efficient agencies to deal with you.'

'That is why I shall now disappear from your lives; fade into the wide, blue yonder where there are no aliens or secret agents expected to chase them.'

'Which is what you always intended to do, isn't it.'

'So, with your permission...'

'I won't stop you.'

Hardly were the words out of Daffy's mouth when the

hammer of the ancient spring gun clicked home. There was a recoil and dull thud followed by a small gasp of surprise from Magin.

Daffy couldn't believe what had just happened. 'Oh my God!'

Magin recovered from his surprise and laughed knowingly. 'I told you, didn't I. Those things are notoriously unstable.'

The thought that she had almost killed someone, even though they deserved to be shot, turned Daffy's stomach. 'But the bullet must have struck you. I'll get a doctor.'

'No. It just grazed me.' Magin brushed the sleeve of his black frock coat as though examining a scuff mark. 'I probably only need a tailor.'

'Are you sure?' Daffy vividly recalled the vicious looking bullet she had loaded into the spring gun. It might have punctured sheet metal, but this agent mostly resembled quicksilver. At least they could both drop the absurd charade that had taken such a toll on Daffy's easy-going nature. Though she believed her adversary had enjoyed it, he at last showed signs of fatigue.

Magin took out his handkerchief, wiped the perspiration from his forehead, and then folded and replaced it. 'I think it would be best for all of us if you went back to the house and forgot everything that has happened.'

'That could take some doing.'

'There is nothing else for it. Few people really believe in aliens, and you wouldn't want to become a focus for all the geeks that do.'

'What will your superiors do to you?'

'Probably retire me. That is why I prefer to leave while I can.'

'Retire you?'

'Oh yes. The department has a place specially reserved for its burnt out agents. Beautiful gardens, luxury facilities, safely tucked away from the prying masses.'

Daffy looked sceptical. 'A place where the occasional graze

can heal - Bruises to the ego can take a little longer. Really not my style.'

'You're not lying this time?'

'Why should I lie?'

'I don't know. Why should you?'

'You are a very perceptive lady, Aunt Daffy. Even if you never manage to work out who I really am, you will be able to live without knowing.'

'I doubt it. If you never become our heartbreak, I'm pretty sure you'll manage to become somebody else's.'

'I was merely fulfilling my function.'

Daffy was puzzled by the enigmatic change in the man. It was as though, now the chase was over, the intellectual engine had powered down into another, stranger, gear. She could believe for a moment that Magin actually understood Life, the Universe, and Everything.

Or perhaps there was another reason. 'You have been hurt, haven't you?'

Magin went to the steps leading down to the overgrown avenue and lowered himself onto their mossy stone. 'No.' Magin's smile had a disconcerting sincerity. 'You should have used a silver bullet. I'm merely tired.'

She felt some irrational sympathy for the man. He looked much older than when they first encountered each other. 'All the same, I'd rather a doctor saw you.'

Magin didn't want to entertain the complications that would cause and waved the suggestion aside. 'Please make sure that Thumper is all right.'

The fright of almost killing someone had made Daffy forget about her niece's sore head, and she hurried off, calling back over her shoulder, 'One of us will come back in a few minutes to make sure you're okay!'

CHAPTER 43

So this was the way it was going to end; with a messy whimper instead of military mobilisation to contain an alien invasion.

There was even no excuse for Colonel Angela Tovey to shoot Magin.

He had lost as well. At least her failure would only warrant a couple of lines on a secret report. God only knew what Magin's department did to its losers. Agents from departments so secret only the sewer rats knew about them, tended to disappear, bones and all. Not even the army was that specialised. Colonel Tovey could eliminate the odd nuisance; the problem was making all trace of them vanish. Anyway, she much preferred to shoot drug runners; nobody cared about where you left their bodies.

As he lounged on the stone steps, Magin heard a woman's voice just above him. 'You let it escape on purpose?'

He didn't look up. 'Ah, at last my shadow speaks.'

Colonel Tovey came down the steps and faced the other agent. 'Very neat solution. Now neither of us gets the alien.'

Magin pushed himself up into a sitting position. 'Does it matter?'

'You great prick! If you hadn't interfered-'

'But I did. You just happened to be following too far behind.'

'You are aware of what we've lost, aren't you?'

'Of course not. Neither are you. It isn't time for the specimens in the zoo to be let loose on the Universe. Leave it a few centuries. Let others come to us and toss peanuts through the bars. Until then, chill out and appreciate the bananas we've already got.'

'You pompous...'

'A little knowledge can be dangerous on an empty brain.' Magin noticed that there was no gun in her concealed holster. 'Am I being paranoid, or were you thinking of using me for target practise as well?'

Colonel Tovey shook the gun free from her sleeve. 'I expected you to be armed.'

'I have no weapon other than my innate wit.'

'You're still a pompous prick.'

'So shoot me.'

This man didn't only play poker, he apparently had a penchant for Russian roulette as well. Nobody, but nobody, ever invited this woman to shoot them, even as a joke.

'Shoot you?'

'If it will help to relieve some hormonal imbalance.' Magin's benign smile was provocation enough in itself.

The military officer reluctantly recalled her orders, if you can't bring in either, "Don't Kill Them!"

'No, I'm not going to shoot you. Keep up that oily charm and someone else will do that sooner or later. I rather think it will be the very people who sent you.' She returned her firearm to its holster. 'So why don't you carry a gun?'

'I don't shoot people, wherever they come from. There is no such thing as an alien, only self-interested points of view.' It sounded like a protest.

'Rot. We've got film of the creatures.'

'Then we must be aliens to them.'

'Tell me that every stranger is a friend we don't know and I really will shoot you.'

'I've no doubt you've shot a great many "friends"?'

'Only drug runners.'

'Why?'

'I'm good at it.' Colonel Tovey began to find the conversation tedious. 'What is it with you? You're too old and experienced to be a foot soldier?' Something occurred to her. She stepped back, mentally bowled over by the thought. 'Of course! You are the spymaster, aren't you?'

Magin's velvet tone refused to sound defensive. 'I didn't get out much. Idle luxury was beginning to pall.'

'Rubbish. For some reason you daren't trust this to one of your underlings, dare you? And that death wish..? It's not just another distraction, is it?'

'Don't try to work it out. The truth would be too much for even your hard view of the world to take.'

'I bet. But I suspect that spymasters who know too much aren't allowed to fade into the background. You'd certainly never manage it. Was that what you were hoping to do?'

Magin gave a wry smile. 'Something like that.'

'Damn shame you won't be making it.' She laughed. 'Don't worry; you're safe enough from us. The military are always too busy preparing for the next deployment to hold grudges.'

'What about the two women?'

'Either of those disappear and too many people would notice. As long as they never find out about me, they're safe enough. Neither are physicists or molecular biologists, so they'll never know what they were really hiding.'

'Neither will we.'

CHAPTER 44

When Daffy got back, Thumper was recovering and well enough to be calling Magin a few choice names.

'What happened?' she demanded as soon as her aunt came into focus.

'Cloval escaped. I don't know how. They must have got a recall unit to her.'

Thumper flopped back in her chair and took a deep breath. 'Well, that's that then.'

'Not quite.' After checking that there were no dogs inside it, Daffy thoughtfully closed the door to the deep freezer. 'There's still Magin.'

'What about him? He can't do anything now. I don't think he's the type that would waste time with revenge.'

'I think I shot him.'

'What?'

'Not deliberately. The gun went off in my hand. It only grazed him.'

Thumper sighed in relief. It would be just as difficult trying to dispose of the body of a secret agent as an alien.

'I said that one of us would go back and see how he was,' Daffy hinted, obviously not wanting to do it herself.

Thumper rubbed her skull ruefully. 'I suppose I ought to. Even if it's only to thank him for the meal last night and lump on my head this afternoon. What sort of mood is he in?'

'Strange. Looks exhausted. You're right, he's probably harmless enough now things are over.'

Thumper wondered if he had really been that dangerous before. If she had scratched the top varnish, she would have probably found he was a little crazed underneath.

She noticed that Daffy was folding a tea towel as though it were a piece of origami. 'What's the matter?'

'I don't know. It's the same feeling I sometimes get about my Christopher.' He had been lost at sea over twenty two years ago and she knew that memories were bound to bother her now and then. It was just that, with some people, it took a long time to believe that they were dead.

'Why think about him now?'

'I sometimes get the feeling that he's still alive.'

'Alive?'

'Not stranded on an island somewhere or married to a mermaid, but in limbo. Perhaps in the desert of water covering most of this planet is "an isle full of noises", a place where dying is a long drawn out process.'

Thumper was unsettled at this uncharacteristic melancholy. 'Knock it off; you're giving me the creeps.'

'Only I can't make out whether Magin is an Ariel or Caliban. A creature trapped for an eternity in the cleft of a tree, or smitten by all the afflictions a monster deserves.'

'Oh Aunt Daffy... tomorrow Magin will be gone for good. Cheer up, you're upsetting the dogs.' Thumper changed the subject. 'We don't have to finish the rest of the carrot pie tonight, do we?'

At the thought of food, Daffy cheered up. 'All right, we'll have something to celebrate.'

Now her aunt had recovered from her strange mood Thumper went into the garden and through to the grounds of the estate beyond. She expected that Magin would have left for another assignment and was surprised to see him still sitting on the mossy steps. He was trying to release a fine silver band underneath the turtleneck of his shirt.

Thumper unfastened the small, intricate catch for him. She removed the device and studied it.

So that's how he did it! Of course he didn't need to carry a mobile - he was wearing a transmitter.

Magin smiled at her annoyance. 'Untrained people don't usually think to search someone's neck.'

Thumper could have kicked herself. As clogs can leave lasting wounds, she sat on the step above the tall agent instead, and looked him in the eye. 'Why do you want to get rid of it now?'

Magin took the narrow band from her. 'Isn't technology remarkable.'

'You don't sound that overwhelmed by it.'

'Oh, I've been thoroughly overwhelmed by technology. I'm sometimes surprised that I don't think with printed circuits.'

'Would you want to?'

'Damn progress! Nature can never be programmed back once she's been scared off.'

Thumper gave a small, gleeful chuckle. 'And I thought it was all an act.'

'I'm tired.' Magin tossed the collar onto a step.

'How long are you allowed out of your burrow?'

'It's too beautiful an afternoon to waste on worrying

157

about that.'

'So the game is over?' she asked warily.

Magin straightened his back into a more comfortable position against one of the balusters. 'Oh yes. In a strange way I enjoyed it.'

'Gave me kittens and a headache.'

'Sorry. I didn't mean to hurt you.'

Thumper chose to believe him on this occasion. 'It's okay. It's something to remember you by.'

'May I have a token to remember you by?' Magin asked.

'Didn't Aunt Daffy let you have a bullet?'

'I'm not sure where that went to.' His gaze fell on Thumper's necklace of pink cowrie shells; it obviously fascinated him.

Never having acquired any great attachment to Mrs Knight's gift, Thumper removed it and gave it to him. Magin looked at the smooth, rounded shells for a moment and then took off the gold pendant he wore.

With some difficulty, he lifted Thumper's frizzy locks and hung it round her neck. 'An exchange.'

'But it's solid gold! I can't take that!'

'I want you to have it. Recompense for the headache.'

After the mean way she had treated him, however admirable the reason, Thumper was uneasy about accepting a 22 carat pendant valuable enough to save her taking out a bank loan and put her ceramics business on a sure footing. There was something uncompromising about the way he gave it, though, and she didn't want to argue with him. He seemed contented enough with the shells.

Thumper had never understood men. They were always doing and saying one thing when really meaning something else.

Magin turned his attention to the sky.

Thumper couldn't make out what was so fascinating about it. 'You should have been a meteorologist.'

'The sky fascinates me.'

'Like flowers and shells?'

'Like trees, meadows, lakes, mountains, wild creatures,

tame creatures, waterfalls...'

'Rainbows?'

'Rainbows?' Magin chuckled. 'What do you know about rainbows?'

'It wouldn't take my weight, and I wouldn't step onto one even if there was a pot of gold at the end of it.'

'Oh how you take so much beauty for granted.'

'How long are you going to stop here?'

Magin's attention remained on the circling swifts.

'As long as it takes.' His voice was barely audible.

'As long as what takes?'

He suddenly realised that she was asking him something. 'Don't let me keep you if you want to go.'

Thumper wanted to ensure that Daffy had snapped out of her odd mood, yet she inexplicably knew that she shouldn't leave. 'Do you want me to stay?'

Magin fixed her with his gleaming amber gaze. 'Would you?'

'If you want. I've only got to get the station wagon back. I can do that tomorrow. Why do you want me to stay?'

'I like company.'

Thumper laughed. This agent was the most solitary, self-reliant individual she had ever encountered, and yet... there was that something about him even she couldn't read. He didn't need to feel wanted. He was one of those rare creatures who could do with or without anyone else; an emotional gyroscope which would always find its centre of gravity. Magin was unlike the people who were forever contemplating their navels and blaming the world for what they were too lazy to work out for themselves.

Thumper marvelled that this man needed to feel wanted. 'How can someone with your remarkable skills not be in demand?'

Magin gave a sour smile. 'Were life that simple. You've no desire to be someone else.'

'You have then? Seems to me you already have everything.'

'Everything?'

'Albeit like a rose bush with the best compost. You just prefer to grow thorns instead of petals. That's your choice.'

The agent shook his head. 'No, think of me every time you pull up a dandelion and, for a second, wonder if there hadn't been some redeeming beauty in its jagged, tiger petals after all.'

Thumper laughed. 'You? A dandelion?'

'I am a dandelion of this Universe. I could have been a useful weed, yet when I bleed people will see a colourless sap.'

Thumper felt uneasy. 'Don't talk like that. It sounds as though you're on about death.'

'All right. I would suffer a million more darts of your venom to die sweetly, though.'

It was all right. The man was only being ironic. 'There is nothing sweet about death. No one's life can be that sour.'

'Not even the weirdest of the weird?'

'I didn't really mean that.'

'I am weird. It takes weird people to do weird jobs.'

Magin's mellowed manner made Thumper feel more uncomfortable than when he was intimidating. Behind the dark amber glow of his eyes was a frightening forest of thought. In some small clearing an atomic clock counted out the atoms in the Universe; in another, wispy butterflies attempted to escape the web of thorny reality.

Magin sensed that the mirrors of his mind were hypnotising Thumper. He closed his eyelids.

As though prodded from behind, he opened them again. She wondered how he managed to sleep without their co-operation.

'Describe a rainbow to me,' he asked.

CHAPTER 45

As Alvas and Mital strode down the slope to the garden boundary they encountered a youth coming from the lift lobby. He was slightly tousled and apprehensive, and clutched a letter that was rolled and sealed with the antique script of ancient nobility.

Alvas was curious. 'Where are you going?' he asked, careful not to use his interrogator's tone on one of his own age-group.

'To the Park Keeper's lodge.' Delas tucked the letter into the sleeve of his overgown. 'Have you finished your interview with Monitor ..?' The words trailed off as though he didn't want to utter the name.

'Our business is now finished,' Mital told him.

'Thank you.'

'Go safely.'

Delas nodded in deference to their seniority, and then dashed on his way.

'Strange,' mused Alvas. 'I have the feeling that something is about to happen.'

Mital gave a faintly sarcastic smile. 'Feelings should not be our burden until we reach the age of majority.'

'Nevertheless, there is something in the air, as though everything we know is about to change.'

'I think you are nearer to your majority than the age scan predicts.'

Alvas smiled. 'Perhaps that is the reason.'

The young couple wended the tortuous, steep way down from the sky top garden, now free to discuss all the elements of the strange case of rebellious travel technicians, secretive scouts, and worlds they would never see. In this instance, "No Further Action" was something to be grateful for.

CHAPTER 46

Thumper and Magin sat on the mossy steps, watching swifts describe eccentric spirals high in the sky as they feasted on insects wafted up on light thermals. Below, the estate's once sweeping grand avenue was now rippling meadowland and the occasional cloud of dandelion seeds appeared above the rim of a nearby ha-ha. House martins dipped to drink from an ornamental lake long since clogged by weed, and a foil crisp packet sailed like a silver duck in the ripples they made. Now and then a toad gave a forlorn croak. Not finding anyone to fight or mate with, it flopped off to its hole in a crumbling wall like a dispirited Don Quixote from where it picked off mayflies. A water vole nuzzled its way through the stream that fed the lake to evict any mouse or amphibian that had taken shelter for the night in its bank side home.

Until then it had not occurred to Thumper how busy Nature could be.

Magin watched in a reverie it would have been churlish to interrupt with conversation. He dreamily murmured the names of passing butterflies and gently swaying flowers and Thumper imagined he would have even identified a dinosaur had that lumbered from the distant mire created by the lack of drainage.

Could anything have been more incongruous than this immaculate secret agent holding solitary court before the procession of Nature's realm like some satanic Oberon? Thumper wasn't so won over that she felt like his Titania. A grumpy Peaseblossom or Mustardseed perhaps, ready to deal with the sort of pubescent Puck who had made her life a misery at school. There were no fairies or hooligans here, though. The only things which screamed were the swifts, and the only things remotely violent were the nettles and ants.

Thumper rubbed the gold pendant against her cheek. It had been like taking sweets without offering any in return. Was this to be the story of her life, or was Magin only a one off? How could she expect to ever meet anyone like him again? Oddly enough, it bothered her. Then she noticed that Magin appeared to be dozing off.

'Are you all right?'

'The sun is making me drowsy.'

'Shall we move now?'

Magin gave a contented smile. 'I want to see the sun go down.'

'Good view from here.'

The shell of this artist's vast heaven slowly rotated, the fluorescing red globe painting the sky with scarlet ribbons of cloud. A full moon was waiting to rise, trailing the bright evening star like a bridesmaid.

Hardly expecting Thumper to have stayed this long, Magin took a small torch from his pocket. 'If you don't go now you may need this to get back.'

'It's all right, I've got one.'

Dusk fell. The gleam in Magin's amber eyes began to fade as though the candle generating it was guttering out with the sinking sun.

Thumper caught a glimpse of Daffy in the distance. Seeing that her niece was safe enough, she returned to the house without disturbing them.

Magin held the cowrie shells to his cheek, comforted by their small, smooth shapes and wound them round his fingers as if defying some demon to snatch them from him.

Thumper once again looked guiltily at the gold pendant and felt nothing.

'What are you thinking about?' she asked.

'The fragrance of moonlight.'

'Moonlight doesn't sme-' She stopped. 'I'm going to buy a telescope when I've paid for the kiln. The sky here can be very clear sometimes – I want to see the Milky Way from end to end.'

'I didn't think that Nature interested you that much?'

'Well, the stars aren't like butterflies and weeds, are they.'

'What have you got against her?'

Thumper shrugged. 'I suppose I believe she let me down.' She gave a puzzled frown at her own revelation. 'Who do you blame for your disappointments?'

'The stars, only the stars.'

'Why?'

'Because they need never mind what I think.'

Thumper was thoughtful for a moment. 'Why do you do it?'

'Do what?'

'Spy or pry, or whatever? You don't really like your job, do you? It must be dangerous.'

'It would take more courage to break free.'

'Why not try?'

'I know too much.'

'Do they know about me and Aunt Daffy?'

'They know nothing which could involve either of you.'

'Thanks... Why not?'

'There would have been no point.' Magin smiled wryly. 'You must forgive me, but I quite like both of you.'

'We forgive you.' Thumper nervously nibbled the medallion. 'I think Aunt Daffy might like you a little. She was really worried when she thought she'd shot you. Death bothers her.'

'It does most people.'

'Not you though? You must be used to the idea.'

'Life has been long enough.'

Suffused with contentment, Magin watched the last swift leave the sky and a darkening warm hue settle on the far horizon. The agent had probably failed an assignment for the first time in his life, only to find peace of mind.

Thumper was both fascinated and puzzled, and wasn't prepared for what came next.

'Make me a promise Thumper.'

'Sure,' she agreed unsuspectingly. 'What is it?'

'Give me your hand.' Thumper put her hand in his. He grasped it firmly. 'Now place your other hand on my jugular veins.'

Thumper was apprehensive, yet nevertheless lifted her fingertips to his throat.

'When you feel the blood cease to flow, you must refasten the silver collar round my neck and push the small green switch by the catch.'

'What!?' Thumper quickly withdrew her hand. She rapidly unfastened the jewelled buttons of his coat.

Over Magin's heart there was a small, deep, hole leaking a trickle of blood through his cream shirt.

CHAPTER 47

The Park Keeper had slipped a sedative into Forram's mulled drink. He now sat back on the cushions, thoughtfully plucking at his mane. How had such a benign person managed to get caught in the cleft of this cruel dilemma? Hopefully, the next person to tackle his job would qualify through lack of compassion. However much Forram had indulged his scouts with luxurious living quarters, the defective ones suffered all the same.

The garden and lodge were so quiet they were able to hear the patter of youthful footsteps outside. Their owner hesitated before coming in. Forram guessed who they belonged to.

He lifted his eyes as though about to drown.

The curtain was drawn aside and a slightly built youth cautiously peered into the lodge.

'Come in lad, come in,' the Park Keeper called out.

Delas cast a glance at the huddled form near the stove, and then turned to face Forram. Drowning or not, the youth's expression suggested that he wouldn't have even thrown his father a straw to clutch at.

Forram looked away from his son's searing gaze.

Satisfied his father felt sufficiently uncomfortable, Delas handed him the sealed letter.

'My mother sent you this note.'

'Thank you son.' Before Forram could look up, Delas had already gone to where D24 lay shivering by the stove.

He carefully rearranged the cloak covering the defective unit as though tending a small child.

Forram read Arbel's letter.

Having reached the end of it, he started to read it again.

CHAPTER 48

Blood from the wound in Magin's chest had somehow been held back by the spring gun's wickedly sharp steel bullet lodged in his heart, and left a dark, meandering stain on his silk shirt. Now Thumper wished that she hadn't despised her mobile quite so much and thought to bring it with her.

She leapt up.

Magin held onto her hand. 'It's too late.'

Thumper was at her wits end. 'How could you sit there for so long without saying anything?'

'There is very little pain.'

'You must have been in agony.'

'Agony is relative. There are far worse ways to die. Those in my profession seldom draw pensions.'

'What sort of agency would inflict a fate worse than dying on its employees like this for failing an assignment?'

'It's not failure they punish, something far more unforgivable.'

'What?'

Magin tapped his ivory forehead. 'My mind isn't what it used to be. When they discover my need to watch birds and butterflies, and wander the countryside on summer nights, they will know that I am beyond hope.'

'Those sentiments are natural in everyone.'

'I wasn't trained to be natural. That is why you must ensure I'm dead before you replace the collar.'

'That's ridiculous!' Thumper tried to free her hand from his vice-like grip. 'Whoever is after you - that's no reason to die. They can't hold you responsible just because we helped Cloval to escape.'

'As soon as you switch the collar on, you must leave immediately... not be seen...' Magin's words trailed off.

On the verge of death, his expression was more peaceful than it had been in life. Only then did Thumper realise that it would be wrong to rob the man of oblivion, or perhaps some strange paradise secret agents escape to.

Magin's long body slowly slid down onto the steps where it lay elegantly sprawled like a fallen swift.

Thumper's hand was released, though his grasp on the cowrie necklace remained tightly closed.

Thumper was astounded.

She had never seen anyone die before and this seemed so tidy and unreal. Magin had managed to do the ultimate in his own no nonsense way as if it were just another facet of his many skills. She sat motionless for what felt like a lifetime.

Magin's eyelids were half open. Thumper wanted to reach out and close them, but if there were a ghost to leave his body, it would be through those amber eyes.

Gingerly Thumper felt Magin's jugular veins. There was no pulse.

Oberon was dead.

She pushed down the neck of his shirt, replaced the fine silver collar and pushed the green switch. Though there was no point to it because his well-behaved hair had not allowed a strand to fall out of place, she combed down his fringe with her fingers and carefully refastened his coat.

Instead of leaving to avoid someone from Magin's department arriving to collect his body, Thumper sat gazing at the lifeless enigma.

When at last able to glance away from his body, she was aware of something glittering above her. A slight figure in a dazzling gown was watching her as though waiting to be invited down from the transmission portal. As he moved towards her, he seemed to float over the crumbling steps as though not quite part of her dimension. Although unlike Cloval in height and demeanour, he was obviously Sovariagn.

Thumper was puzzled. Now Cloval had escaped, the aliens should have learnt their lesson and left Earth well alone.

Then she realised. Cloval must have told them about the agent pursuing her.

The glittering visitor looked at the body sprawled out on the steps and Thumper moved away from Magin.

Like a benevolent wizard, the alien raised his hands. A web of light cocooned Magin. The agent's body gently rose, his frock coat flapping as he floated up the steps and through the transmission portal.

Thumper watched the magical scene in a silence. With a sudden ripple of light, Magin and the alien disappeared.

Thankfully, when the agent from his department came there would be no body to collect, which meant that Aunt Daffy could not be accused of killing the man.

CHAPTER 49

Forram read Arbel's letter yet again.

'What's wrong?' demanded the Park Keeper.

Forram's skin became eerily pallid and there was a catch in his voice. 'I'm not sure.' He read the letter aloud.

"Forram beloved, this is the last token of my love you will ever receive. Life for me has no meaning while you are tortured by guilt and reviled by our son.

"My actions may seem irrational to you at first, but remember, I was also party to the destruction of a noble and gentle creature.

"You have always been right; scouts do feel joy and anguish. After burning out D24's implants as though they were diseased legions, I can no longer doubt it. I know it is impossible to save the unit from lingering until its natural death, yet I must be sure that nothing like this can ever happen again..."

Forram allowed the letter to fall to his lap, hardly daring to understand its meaning. The Park Keeper's expression told him she had already reached the same conclusion.

It was too late to dash down to the lightning chamber far below in the citadel.

Forram rose, trance like, from the cushions.

The terrible vacuum which precedes the most fearful sound on the planet filled the Park Keeper's lodge, gardens, and all the land about the shining metropolis. The gong, not rung for so many generations, now pealed out its unworldly message of mortal sacrifice to change a law.

Unsure what was happening, Delas threw his arms about D24's neck and clung to the unit.

Forram just stood, swaying slightly.

The Park Keeper caught him before he fell.

All the defective scouts in the garden hastened back to the safety of the lodge.

The citizens of the metropolis below thronged the pavements, while the gong's voice still reverberated.

The only creature that did not react was D24.

The unit remained huddled in the arms of Delas, fitfully running a necklace of pink cowrie shells through its long fingers.

THE END

www.ingramcontent.com/pod-product-compliance
Lightning Source LLC
Chambersburg PA
CBHW060822120626
46557CB00001B/321